A Thousand Masks

A Thousand Masks

Gina E. Matteson

Sisters Three Publishing

Copyright © 2022 by Gina E. Matteson

All rights reserved. No part of this book may be reproduced, scanned, or transmitted in any printed, electronic, mechanical, including photocopying, recording, or any information storage and retrieval system, without permission in writing from the publisher. Please do not participate in or encourage piracy of copyrighted materials in violation of the author's rights.

The contents of this book were inspired by true events. However, the author and publisher have made every effort to change the names and identifying details of the characters.

Cover art by: Eric Langlois

ISBN: 978-1-0879-8251-9

PRINTED IN THE UNITED STATES OF AMERICA

"…harassment is not about attraction or desirability. It is about exerting power over people whenever you want."
–Feminista Jones

Acknowledgments

With my deepest gratitude, I wish to thank everyone who has come into my life in various ways and formed different relationships with me. There are those who taught me invaluable life lessons about unconditional love, friendship, trust, and hope. For even when I was at my lowest, I always had someone who cared about me and for that, I am eternally grateful.

I would also like to express my love and gratitude to my entire family for always being my biggest source of support and for always lifting me up and believing in me and all my dreams. A special *thank you* for the love that always came from my sister, Lisa. Our eternal bond means the world to me.

To my mother, you truly are my soulmate, and I will love and cherish our bond forever. Your unwavering love and support throughout my entire life guided me through every turn and kept me *Forever Young*.

To my loving husband, Gary. Thank you for always believing in me and encouraging me to follow my dreams and listen to my heart. Your patience, unconditional love, and trust in me have been my lifeline through this process.

You are the man of *my* dreams and the best father I could have ever hoped for. *You & Me, Me & You.*

Most importantly, to my two young children, Connor and Charlotte, you saved my life in ways I'll never completely understand. You showed me the magnificent bond between a child and a mother. The love I have within for the two of you is unconditional and I promise to love and protect you with all that I am. Throughout every stage of our life journey I will always be your biggest supporter.

To my publisher, Caroline Smith from Sisters Three Publishing for your magnificent support and divinity. Thank you for believing in my book, and for helping me share Anastasia's story with the world.

Introduction

People say there are points in your life that are so impactful, they can change the trajectory of your life, and this is true for Anastasia Rose. This story is about love, betrayal, forgiveness, family, empowerment, and learning to love again. Through Anastasia's story, you'll see the effects of what happens to many young girls who begin their life with betrayal and abuse. Ana's story shows us the truth we don't want to face and sometimes completely block from our memory. This coping mechanism can be divine until the day…you do remember.

Each year, millions of children are sexually abused, many by close family members. There is less danger in stranger interactions than we might want to believe. Most child predators know their victims.

Ana's story reveals the shame these children hide inside, the true effects it can have throughout the child's entire life. Child sexual abuse impacts lifelong health and well-being, and it shapes everything about the individual, whether they know it or not. Showing unconditional love to someone who has been betrayed rarely helps if they can't love themselves. This is a very difficult and sensitive path to navigate. Having people who will walk this path with you, can save you but most importantly, you can and have to save yourself.

There are victims and there are survivors. Ana's story allows us a glimpse into the ugly truth that lives in many homes that go undetected. This book will remove the blinders so we can finally see how this betrayal truly affects our younger generation and why it's so important to be aware of the signs and the immense importance of not ignoring them.

My goal for writing this book is to ensure every family and child knows they are not alone and to empower survivors to know that you do not need to be silent, ashamed, or feel guilty.

This book also is about empowering women to know their value and to not accept anything less than the love you deserve, the kind of love that doesn't hurt but rather makes you feel loved and safe. This book will show you there is *hope*, that comes in many different shapes, forms, and bonds. Women do not need to be silent anymore, we can speak our truth, I hope this book shows you that you deserve the best that life has to offer but you must know your worth and work towards self-discovery and most importantly, self-love. This is a lifelong journey; I hope this book helps you to understand that you are never truly alone.

PART I:
Hiding in Plain Sight

Chapter 1

The room was still but for the soft ticking of the clock. The breeze blowing through the bedroom window hinted that summer was making its way into fall. Feeling the chill, Anastasia Rose snuggled deeper into the quilt her grandmother had sewn for her. She dreamed about what the season would bring. Maple Ridge celebrated fall with bonfires and caramel apples. Family festivals played music, and crafters sold colorful mittens and hats for the upcoming winter.

Ana loved autumn for its cozy clothes, hot chocolate, and all the excuses it gave her to cuddle up close to her mom. This was the start of the holiday season when all the cousins in her family would come to town, and they'd go to the festivals, parties, and events together. Ana loved the family gatherings for Halloween, Thanksgiving, and Christmas, but she most loved the time it gave her with her best friend: her grandpa. He always made her feel happy and safe, and he was the coolest grandfather in the whole world.

The familiar smell of pancakes wafted through the open bedroom door, and Ana's tummy growled. Half-awake, she jumped out of bed and raced across her room, bumping into her desk on the way out the door.

"Ouch!"

Her heavy red toolbox fell off the desk, tools scattering all around her. She winced as a long, silver wrench landed on her foot. She picked it up and looked at it. It was a gift from her grandpa. She held it for a moment, thinking of him.

"What a strange gift for a six-year-old girl," Mom had said. But Ana knew how much it meant to him. He was teaching her how to fix things, and the wrench was his way of reminding her of their time together. Ana was a girly girl, but she loved that her grandpa chose her to help tinker on his projects. She'd once been jealous of how close her older sister, Avery, was to their grandma. But now, she had grandpa's full attention.

She carefully replaced all the tools and raced down the stairs. Avery was already at the kitchen table, a perfect, round pancake on the plate in front of her.

"Good morning!" Mom said in her usual musical way. Ana sat and reached for the half-full glass of milk Mom had poured. It was family time, which meant no distractions allowed—no beeping phones, no chirps. It was just the three of them sharing their daily adventures and stories.

Ana loved these times around the table with her family. Mom was often busy with university and work. Yes, she was always home in time to make dinner, help with homework, and tuck her into bed, but Saturday morning breakfast was special family time.

"Mom, what was it like when you were a girl? Did Grandma make you pancakes too?" Ana asked. Sophia frowned slightly and didn't answer. Ana noticed so she shifted her eyes away, sorry she'd asked. Her mom never spoke of her time when she was young. *Maybe she had a secret*, Ana thought, hoping that one day, when she was old enough, Mom would share.

Ana scarfed down her breakfast and rushed out, bursting through the front door, ready to start her day's adventures. But Avery didn't follow. Ana looked back to see she was still at the open door with her usual worried look.

Sophia came up behind Avery and whispered something Ana couldn't hear. Finally, Avery smiled and stepped outside.

"Come on! What's taking you so long?" Ana said, dashing down the driveway.

"Don't go walking around the block! Stay where I can see you," Sophia shouted.

The sun was high in the British Columbia sky, gleaming glorious rays of warmth on Ana's skin. The air was filled with laughter from the neighborhood kids who were already out playing, shouting, and having fun. Within minutes, she was four feet up in the tall oak by their kitchen window, looking down at her sister.

"Be careful, Ana! You're going to fall!" Avery said. Ana just laughed and climbed even higher, not worrying about falling or her sister's nervous voice. Ana knew Avery preferred it when they just laid on the grass with their heads touching, watching the clouds go by.

"Look, Avery! That one's a daddy chicken going home to his family!"

"Yes, he's even got a briefcase!" Avery said. "We should go back inside and start getting ready. Mom said grandma and grandpa are coming today."

"Oh yes! I can't wait!" Ana replied. "I want to show grandpa how well I looked after my toolbox!"

Ana saw Avery roll her eyes, but she didn't care. She and Grandpa would work in the garage together, and he would show her his next big project.

"Anything can be fixed," he would say as they got to work. He always promised that he would one day let her help fix up the old car in their garage. She had been doing her stretches so she could grow tall enough to reach inside without a stool. Maybe today was the day!

When they got inside, they found Mom baking brownies for their grandparent's visit. Ana tried to sneak a piece from the stack cooling on the counter.

"I knew the smell would bring you home," Mom said, shooing her away. "It's like a silent alarm for you and your sister!"

"No, Mom. I came to see you because I love you so much. You're the best mommy ever!" Ana's emerald green eyes gleamed as she teased. Mom knew the real reason she was acting so nice. She was surprised when Mom knelt and put her hands on Ana's cheeks.

"Ana, you and your sister are my most precious gifts." She pinched Ana's nose. "Even though I know you are just saying that for a brownie!" She handed Ana a brownie, and as she took it, she thought she saw a little tear glittering in her mother's eye. Then Ana heard the low rumble of a car in the driveway.

"They're here!" she squealed with excitement, but Avery let out a deep breath as if she'd been holding it in.

After welcoming hugs and kisses, Ana and Avery opened the presents their grandparents had brought. Sophia went to make dinner and Grandma followed behind. Avery went along to have "big girl" conversations that poor little Ana wouldn't understand. She didn't mind because that meant she could have grandpa all to herself.

"You know that old car in your Mama's garage?" he asked. He'd leaned down close to her face. She thought his breath smelled a little funny, but she'd decided it was just "grandpa smell."

Ana nodded.

"How about you help me get started on it, Ana-Cakes?" he said.

Ana didn't say a word as she ran to the garage door, proud that she was grown-up enough to be grandpa's assistant. As they worked, Grandpa told her stories about what life was like when he was a six-year-old. She loved how he trusted her enough to share his secrets.

"Ana, hand me that wrench there," he said, and she was happy to oblige. When Sophia called them for dinner,

Ana watched grandpa roll out from under the car on his funny mechanic's board contraption. She put out her hand to help him up. His greasy fingers intertwined with hers, and they held hands all the way to the kitchen. Ana didn't even mind how long it took to wash the grease off.

* * *

"My favorite fish fry, Sophia! Thank you!" Grandpa said, pushing back from the table.

Ana was sleepy from lunch but also from Avery sharing all the little details about her play at school. When Grandpa put out his hand, Ana didn't waste a minute taking it and following him toward the garage. She looked back at the ladies at the table. She'd rather hang out with grandpa and tinker than listen to another Avery story for the millionth time.

Time flew by. Before they knew it, it was time for Ana and Avery to go to bed. Whenever their grandparents came to visit, the girls slept together in Ana's room. Usually, it would feel like a huge deal to have to give up part of her bed for her sister, but tonight Ana felt like a little company wouldn't be such a bad thing. The day had been warm and bright, but the windows had been closed and the room felt eerily cold. But more than that, something felt out of place.

"It feels funny in here," she said to Avery, who didn't reply.

One thing was for sure: Avery was acting very strange, and Ana couldn't understand why. Normally, Avery's constant babble and chatter filled the room, but not tonight. Ana wanted to say something but felt afraid to—as if something bad would happen if she said a single word.

Finally, she couldn't take it anymore. "What's wrong?" she asked, taking a big gulp of air.

"Oh . . ." Avery said. "It's probably nothing."
"Come on then! Spit it out! Tell me!" Ana felt a shiver that wasn't from the cold.
"Ana, you can't tell anyone I said this . . ." Avery said. Ana waited while Avery stammered and paused.
"Well, I . . . sometimes, I feel a little bit uncomfortable around Grandpa."
Ana stared at her sister. "Why?"
"I don't know," Avery said. "It's confusing."
Ana wanted to push her for more, but Avery clamped her mouth shut, got into bed, and closed her eyes. When she peeked and saw Ana was still staring, she turned her back. It was clear to Ana that the conversation was over for Avery.
"What do you mean?" Ana asked her sister one last time, but Avery ignored her. She felt a strange knot in her stomach, and worry made it hard to fall asleep. She didn't have her usual good dreams that night. Ana was normally a very happy morning person but not this time. Today she woke up groggy and in a terrible mood; scared and confused. Something was wrong. Everything about the morning looked the same as yesterday. It was bright and sunny and children played outside. But to Ana, everything felt different. Breakfast seemed to take longer than usual, and neither Avery nor Ana chattered away like they normally would. Ana squirmed in her seat.
"Didn't you girls sleep well?" grandma asked, her voice full of concern. Both nodded, but they didn't look up from their plates.
"Girls, manners," Mom said.
"Bad dream . . ." Avery said.
"Me too," Ana said.
"Oh, my babies!" Sophia said as she headed toward her daughters. Sitting between them so she could hug them both, she reassured them, "It was just a dream; it's

all over now. You don't have to be scared!" and then she kissed both her girls on their noses.

"Ana, why don't you help grandpa with the car again today? You love that, don't you?" Grandma said. But this time, Ana wished she could stay at the table and listen to the ladies' gossip.

When he stood up and held out his hand, Ana followed her grandfather to the garage. She sat on a tire and watched as he inspected under the hood of the car.

"Now, Ana-Cakes," he said. "What does a carburetor do?"

The nickname she loved yesterday didn't feel so good today.

"Of course, why would you know?" he said when she didn't answer. He let out a long and loud laugh. He sat on the edge of the car and lifted Ana onto his lap, gripping her by the middle.

"Okay, Miss Sensitive! Forget the carburetor! What does a wrench do? I told you this one, remember?" he asked, giving her a tiny shake. His voice was firm and a little scary.

Ana looked at him. "It fixes things," she said almost in a whisper.

Grandpa smirked, clutching her tiny waist even tighter. When she let out the faintest whimper, it was smothered right away.

And then there was silence.

CHAPTER 2

Darkness enveloped her and filled every corner of the room. The air felt cold; there was no breeze, yet her hair floated around her like a halo. Shuddering, she hugged herself tightly, looking around, trying to find light or warmth—anything to make the goosebumps go away. It was cold . . . so cold . . .

In the distance, a faint glow floated. She reached out her hand. Was she just imagining it, or was there warmth out there? It felt so out of reach, but if she just took a few steps more, she'd be able to feel it. Two steps forward . . . reach . . . nothing . . . Another two steps forward . . . reach . . . still nothing. Her breaths came faster the more she stretched her fingertips.

She found herself breaking into a jog, her hands outstretched and chasing the light. With every step, the light seemed to get farther away. Tears fell down her face, her body hurting from the cold; she was out of breath and panting heavily.

How was she moving yet going nowhere? She couldn't stop. She had to keep going. The warmth was so close. Her little six-year-old body felt so heavy. Mustering the last bit of her strength, she broke into a sprint, one hand clenched at her side while the other was outstretched. The warmth tickled her fingertips.

Then a shadow appeared in front of her. His familiar scent of car oil and metal made her want to vomit. It was just his silhouette, but it stopped her cold. Slowly, he walked into her field of vision, covering the light and blocking its warmth, leaving her in darkness once again.

In slow motion, she found herself falling. She covered her eyes, waiting for the inevitable blow of the floor below her. But it never came.

Ana sat up, stifling her scream. She could feel her hair stuck to her neck. She was drenched in sweat. She wiped her forehead with the back of her hand as her eyes adjusted to the dim light of her room. The moon shone high in the sky, and there was absolute silence outside the open window. Growing up in Vancouver, she was used to goose bumps from the cold and rain, but this was different. Deeper.

"It's just a dream," she told herself, over and over. "No. It's just a nightmare."

It had been the same dream for years now, coming every few days and waking her up at the same time of night. Each one felt like the first time though, and she'd sit up wondering why it frightened her so much. She wasn't afraid of the dark. At twelve years old, she considered herself very brave. Though the same intense fear woke her up all those nights, the memory of the nightmare would disappear too quickly for her to grasp.

Ana stretched her sore arms. It felt like she'd been clenching them in real life just as she did in the dream. Yawning, she could feel her eyes getting heavy again. Knowing what an important day it was tomorrow, she wanted to get back to sleep as soon as possible. Laying her head on her pillow, Ana looked out her window at the perfect view of the midnight sky. Bathed in the glow of the moonlight, Ana closed her eyes and fell back to sleep.

Early the next morning, Ana woke to Avery waltzing into her room dressed in her finest Sunday dress.

"Aren't you up yet?" Avery asked. "How do you not suffocate when you lay like that with your face in the pillow? It's time to wake up!"

Ana didn't answer.

Avery went to the closet and pulled out clothes for Ana, laying them at the foot of Ana's bed.

"No wonder Mom calls you a 'mini-mommy'," Ana said after taking a quick glance at Avery's choice of clothes. She rolled over, trying to ignore her sister.

"Come on, Ana! Dad will be here soon!" Avery said. "We're going to brunch with Dad and Trisha!"

Ana and Avery both loved their dad and their stepmom, Trisha, who treated them as if they were her own daughters. Ana was happy to be seeing them today, and besides, brunch was always awesome. She got up and walked past Avery without a word.

"Hurry up!" Avery called down the hall. "I don't want to keep them waiting. I have to talk to Dad about my birthday present."

Ana took her time in the bathroom. When she came out, she paused at the door to watch her sister circling around her room. Avery was straightening up. She picked up some cushions that had dropped on the floor. Bending down, she grabbed a doll that was half-hidden under the bed. Ana held her breath. She saw the confusion on Avery's face. The doll had once been beautiful, but its golden locks were now a mangled mess, chunks of it jaggedly cut and pieces ripped out. And the doll had on way too many clothes. Ana knew how weird it looked. She took a deep breath and walked into the room.

"How can you be so careless with your things? Mom works so hard for us," Avery said.

Ana held her silence.

Avery sighed. "I hope you don't get in trouble."

Ana shrugged.

"Anyway, I got your clothes out for you," Avery said, pointing to the foot of the bed. Ana looked at the outfit she had laid out. She shook her head at the pretty dress and went to her closet to search for something else. She ripped through everything in her closet, but nothing looked right, and panic surfaced inside Ana.

Avery got up from the bed. "Would you please hurry? I'm going downstairs."

Ana abandoned her search and followed her sister down the stairs at a distance and just sat on the stairs. She watched as Avery joined her mother on the porch. Somehow, she felt distant from them, set apart and alone. Ana knew her mother had been especially busy lately, and she was probably looking forward to a bit of a break while the girls spent the day with their dad. Avery was preoccupied with her sixteenth birthday and was thilled that she'd soon be driving and more independent. None of that explained how Ana felt, though.

"Mom?" Ana heard Avery say. "Do you like my dress?" She twirled to give their mother a full view of her outfit. "You look absolutely beautiful, my darling," Mom replied. "When did you become such a grown-up?"

The familiar rumbling of Dad's car coming up the street jolted Ana. She bolted up the stairs and dressed as fast as she could.

"Ana!" Sophia shouted.

"Coming!" Ana replied as she scrambled downstairs. Her mother caught her as she tried to run past.

"Hang on, missy. Aren't you going to say goodbye to me?"

Ana didn't reply and kept her head low.

"What's wrong, honey?" Sophia asked. "You haven't been your usual ray of sunshine!"

Ana watched Avery, running down the driveway toward her dad.

Sophia gasped when she noticed what Ana chose to wear today. "Ana, you're going to be hot in all those clothes," she said, pulling at Ana's turtleneck. "It's summer, Ana."

Before her mom could finish her sentence, Ana responded. "No, I won't."

"Why do you have so many layers, Ana? It's hot out!" Sophia asked.

"I'm cold, Mom," Ana replied and quickly kissed her mom on the cheek, hoping she would not worry too much about her fashion choices, then took off running for her dad's waiting car before her mom could say anything else.

That week, Ana stayed busy with school and all the extra-curricular activities that filled her days. By the time Friday came, she felt like she deserved a break.

"My little genius," Sophia would call her, which made Ana feel good. Sitting at the kitchen table, she listened to Avery chatter about her own busy schedule and her sixteenth birthday party, which was only a day away.

Watching Sophia make Avery's birthday cake, Ana felt a drowsy peaceful feeling.

"Darn it!" Sophia said. "I turned the oven on a half-hour ago, and it's stone cold."

"Uh-oh," Ana said.

"Don't you worry, girls. I've got my go-to superhero to take care of it!"

Ana swallowed hard. She watched her mother grab the phone. "Dad! The oven isn't working. Can you come over?" Ana could hear the slight panic in her voice. She knew Mom was stressed with so much to do before the party.

Ana's peaceful feeling fled. She went into the living room and turned on the TV. An hour later, when there was a knock on the door, Ana kept her eyes glued to the screen. She was determined not to be the one to answer it, but no one went to the door. Sophia was busy in the kitchen, and Avery was on the phone with her best friend. Ana kept her eyes glued to the TV, ignoring the persistent knocking.

There was another knock. Ana kept her eyes fixed straight, trying to pretend she had not heard anything. Then another knock. Sighing loudly, she got up and walked toward the door. Maybe it was a pizza, she thought optimistically, grasping the doorknob and turning it slowly.

When she opened the door, she saw Grandpa's familiar face. His tall frame filled the doorway. "Ana-Cakes!" he said, smiling his wide, crooked smile. He opened his arms to her. Startled, Ana stepped backward, but not fast enough. She felt her grandpa's arms envelop her in an embrace.

Ana squirmed away, feeling warm despite the chill in the air.

"Hi, Grandpa," she said, relieved when Avery appeared. Grandpa's gaze left Ana.

"Hello, Avery," he said with a smile. To Ana, it sounded different from how he had greeted her.

"Hi, Grandpa. Are you here to fix the oven?" Avery asked. She sounded polite but Ana knew she was eager to get back to her call. Ana and Grandpa followed Avery to the kitchen where Sophia was now elbow-deep in bread dough.

Grandpa mumbled something gruffly but avoided making eye contact.

"Hi, Dad! The oven is ready for you." Sophia had to shout over the music she loved to play when she was cooking. Before someone asked her to help, Ana ducked out of the room and retreated to the comfort of the sofa. Avery hung around before directing her attention to her phone and joining Ana on the couch in the living room.

After thirty minutes of tinkering, the oven was back in working order.

"There you go, my lady," Grandpa said in a regal fashion.

Sophia laughed. "Thanks, Dad."

"Anything for you, my princess."

"Well, actually Dad, if you don't mind," Sophia hesitated, "there's a whole shelving unit in the living room that needs assembling. I was going to do it before the party but I'm running out of time."

"You got it," Ana heard Grandpa say.

"I'll ask one of the girls to help you, Dad."

With that, Ana made herself scarce, retreating to her bedroom.

"Ana!" her mother called. "Grandpa needs his little helper!"

But Ana didn't leave the room. She listened to her mother's footsteps stalking the house.

"There you are, Avery!" Mom said. Ana was relieved Avery hadn't left the couch. She couldn't hear Avery's reply, but her mother said, "Looks like you get to help Grandpa today."

Ana crept down the stairs to listen to Avery and Grandpa awkwardly talk. Ana knew Avery had little in common with him. But she politely told him about the cheer team she had joined and what her classes were like. Ana figured they'd be building shelves for a while so she returned to the safety of her room. It was a half-hour later when she peeked into the living room. The shelves were finally starting to take shape.

"Avery, why don't you grab that chair and put this top piece on the shelf?" Grandpa said. He handed her a big piece of wood. Avery dutifully did as she was told, climbing up on the chair while he held it in place.

Ana watched her sister balance carefully with her butt out and her chest forward, wrapping herself around the thick shelf so she could hoist it onto the top of the unit. Ana held her breath. The space was tight. Avery had to adjust herself into an awkward position to place the shelf properly. Ana hoped she wouldn't fall. But then, Ana noticed something even worse than that. Her grandfather's eyes were where they shouldn't have been; they were focused on her sister's butt. Ana froze in place. Grandpa didn't break his gaze, and she was sure she saw his lip quiver. She tried to shake those terrible thoughts out of her mind. But then Avery turned to look over her shoulder, and she saw Grandpa looking too.

Avery gasped and scrambled to get down from the chair, obviously wanting to get far away from him. But he reached up and wrapped his hands around her waist. Ana thought maybe he was just trying to help Avery down, but the look on her sister's face told her it didn't feel good. Avery squirmed, but he didn't let go.

"Grandpa!" she said.

"I don't want you to fall," he said in a low voice. Then his hand moved lower, down her back and to her bottom. It lingered. Ana blinked her eyes. *Was he rubbing Avery's butt?*

Avery pushed him away and jumped to the floor, blushing as she ran out past Ana. Moments later, Sophia found Ana standing frozen in the hall. She patted Ana's arm. "You okay, honey?" she asked. Not waiting for an answer, she walked into the living room to marvel at the newly installed shelving.

"Looks great, Dad! Thanks!" she said, hugging her father tightly. "Listen, dinner is almost ready. Why don't you stick around and have dinner with me and the girls?"

"Sure honey, that'll save me having to drive home hungry," he said. "I'll go take a look at that car. Call me when dinner's ready." He kissed his daughter on the cheek and turned on his heel and headed towards the garage.

He brushed past Ana on his way to the garage. He glanced down but didn't say a word. Ana ran up the stairs to her room and shut the door. She crawled under the bed and started counting to one hundred. She always counted to one hundred when she needed to calm down. After her fifth time of counting, her heart was still beating loudly.

"Ana . . ." her mother called from downstairs.

"Eighty-one . . . eighty-two . . . eighty-three . . ."

"Ana!" Sophia called again, this time from the stairwell.

"Ninety . . . ninety-one . . . ninety-two . . ." Ana whispered to herself.

"Ana, where are you?" her mom shouted, concern in her voice. She was getting closer.

"Ninety-eight . . . ninety-nine . . . one hundred."

Her bedroom door swung open, and though Ana knew it was her mom, it startled her.

"Ana!" Sophia said, half-relieved, half-angry. "What are you doing under there?"

Ana was stuck now. How could she answer that question without it leading to more questions? She chose to escape from her safe space and act like nothing was wrong. *Play pretend and it will all be okay*, she thought to herself. She rolled out from under the bed, giggled, and hugged her mom.

"I love you, Mom!" she said, wrapping her petite little arms around her mother. Just like that, Sophia warmed up and hugged her back.

"Honey, I have great news! Grandpa is staying for dinner with us tonight!"

Ana took a deep breath, inhaling the comforting smell of dinner from Sophia's apron.

"He's tinkering with the car, so why don't you go help him before dinner is ready?" Sophia said. She took Ana by the hand and began walking her downstairs. Ana didn't resist. There was no use. She had no way to excuse herself without raising questions. So off she went, hand in hand with her mother. In her head, she kept repeating, *Play pretend and it will all be okay*.

In the garage, that familiar smell of oil and dirt filled her nostrils. Was the garage always this dim, or was it just her eyes playing tricks? Ana squinted; she swore she'd never seen the light so low before. Grandpa always insisted the light be bright so they could see everything. His legs stuck out from under the car. She could hear him whistling a tune to one of his favorite songs.

"Grandpa," she said as she made her way into the garage. His whistling stopped.

"Just a minute, Ana-Cakes."

He made his way out from under the car covered in the usual grease and beamed up at her. She stared at his dirt-stained hands. Those hands had taught her so much; now the sight of them made her feel sick. Grandpa got up, teetering a little, and hugged her, being careful not to get grease on her. He handed her a flashlight and made his way to the front of the car.

"Shine the light right there for me," he said. "That's good."

She did as she was told. As they had done many times before, they started talking about why classic cars were great.

Time flew by, and Ana relaxed. She even shared with grandpa her hopes of being able to win her race at the school's upcoming Field Day. She was halfway through her story about her theory on how she could run faster when grandpa angrily shouted and kicked the car's tire.

"What's wrong?" she asked, startled at his reaction.

"It's the damn wrench!" he growled. "I've dropped it in there, and my arms are too big to get it."

She could hear how annoyed he was. Ana instinctively offered to help. "I can get it for you, Grandpa," she said, putting her flashlight down.

She came next to him and peered under the hood. She pressed her stomach onto the cold metal and arched herself forward to reach in. She could see the wrench caught in a tight space, but her arms were just a little too short.

She pulled herself higher up into the car. Suddenly, she could feel him press himself up against the lower half of her body, pressed up enough to where she could feel every detail of him. Her mind went blank. Her body went cold, cold like in her dreams. His hands, dirty and oily, swept her hair away from her neck. Her neck was exposed to the cold air that swept around her; she shivered. His hands gripped her, stroking her back and making her feel colder. A wave of nausea invaded Ana's stomach. He pressed himself tighter to her. She closed her eyes and started to count. *Play pretend*, she thought. She felt his lips close to her neck and his dirty hands moving down her petite body. *Play pretend*, she thought again, *and it will all be okay.*

* * *

The house was filled with noise and laughter. Kids were running around chasing each other, parents chatted with their drinks in hand, and teenagers darted around the edges of the room acting way too cool. Ana was sitting on the staircase, eyes red from crying.

It had been a rough morning. Sophia had tried to force her to wear a party dress that Grandma and Grandpa had bought for her, but she'd refused, insisting that her dark black jeans, long-sleeve turtleneck, and thick coat were party-ready. Her mom had told her she would be boiling in it, but Ana insisted she would be comfortable. It turned into an epic argument, and Sophia had ended up backing down, but only after Ana had begun her loud and deep sobbing.

"I'm not having this, Ana; you will not stress me out today!" Sophia had shouted before putting the party dress back in her daughter's wardrobe and storming out.

Now Ana was sitting on the stairs in a self-imposed exile, refusing to join in on the festivities and play with her cousins, which was always her favorite part of family gatherings. Avery was standing with her best friends; *she's probably talking about makeup and boys*, Ana thought. Not everyone had arrived, but the house was getting busy.

"Ana, come play with us!" Shannon shouted from across the room. Shannon was one of Ana's favorite cousins, probably because she reminded Ana a lot of herself when she was six years old. Shannon reached her tiny hands out to her cousin and Ana took them, letting Shannon draw her into a game of tag.

Come on, Ana. Just have fun, she told herself. She wanted to forget what happened in the garage and feel like one of the kids again.

Soon, the party was in full swing. Ana loved it when her family got together. Though she was a little older than many of her cousins, Ana still enjoyed being a kid and playing silly games. It brought back the carefree spirit of her six-year-old self. Sophia often had to remind her that twelve years old was by no means old, but Ana was convinced she was basically an adult now.

Later that afternoon, Ana fell on the floor in a fit of giggles in the midst of dancing with Shannon. Her cousin, James, had just finished teaching them a cool dance the kids at his school were doing. None of them seemed particularly good at it. At one point, Ana had caught a glimpse of herself in the mirror with her tongue sticking out and her face confused, trying to follow James' directions.

Taking a momentary break from the fun, Ana made her way to the drinks table and grabbed a soda. She looked back at her cousins, now playing a new game where Shannon was the question master. Ana felt her heart soar. It had been a long time since she had felt this happy. She looked around the room. Avery was talking to a boy she had a crush on as their friends surrounded them on either side. Her mom was exchanging stories with her aunts and uncles. Her dad and Trisha sat on the sofa with a few other relatives. The house was full, heaving with noise and people. It was the happiest Ana could remember it being.

Then, like a cloud covering sunshine, she heard Grandpa walk in with Grandma as everyone went to greet them with their usual hugs and kisses. The room went silent even though she could see people still talking. Her ears burned, her throat dried, and her smile disappeared. Of course, she knew he was coming, but he was late. She was grateful for it, even hoped at one point he wouldn't come at all. Then, he was standing in the middle of the room, sucking up all the air from her lungs.

He hadn't spotted her yet, and she didn't intend for him too. She put herself out of his view. He made his way to Avery, Grandma tailing after him. They wished her a happy birthday and gave her a gift, but when Grandpa leaned in to kiss her, Avery flinched. As they walked away, Ana caught her wiping his kiss off her cheek. No one else noticed, but Ana certainly did.

No longer feeling in the party mood, Ana made her way into the garage and hid inside the car.

* * *

She didn't know how long she'd been asleep when she was jolted awake by the light in the garage. Ana stayed still, waiting to see who had come in.

"When I'm finished with this car, it will be the most beautiful car on the road," Grandpa said to his unknown companion. "Who would like to help me fix it up?" he asked.

Ana heard the voices of Shannon and her little cousin Lacey, who was only five years old. Their voices rose, competing for Grandpa's attention.

"I'm older than you, Lacey. I get to help Grandpa out first!" Shannon insisted, with force in her voice.

Ana felt her blood run cold. He was here in this garage with two of her young, sweet, and innocent cousins, and they had no clue what would happen if they stayed.

"It's not fair that you get to help first just because you're older, Shannon," Lacey said. "I'm going to tell my mom!" She stomped her foot and ran out of the garage, leaving Grandpa and Shannon alone. Ana was afraid to make a sound. Grandpa and Shannon carried on talking, but then she heard something in Grandpa's voice change.

"Let me lift you to look inside the hood," he said. "You're still too short to see in by yourself."

Ana had a vague memory of him saying the same thing to her. She hoped she was wrong in how she remembered the details of what happened next: the unwelcome touches and searching hands from a man she was supposed to be able to trust. Bile rose up in her throat.

Ana sat straight up and clearly startled Grandpa, who moved quickly away from Shannon. His face was that of a guilty man caught in the act.

Shannon beamed at Ana. "Where have you been?" she asked in a playfully disapproving tone.

Grabbing Shannon's hand, Ana pulled her cousin away from the car. Ana's eyes burned as they met her grandfather's. He looked both furious and afraid at the same time as he had never seen this side of Ana before. Ana felt the weight of the world on her shoulders. She'd have to walk back into the party as if nothing had happened. Her grip on Shannon's hands tightened. Her small cousin had no clue, no idea, and Ana told herself she would make sure Shannon would never find out what Ana had just saved her from.

"Come on, Shannon. Let's get some cake, huh?" Sweat beaded on her forehead as her grandfather watched her take Shannon from the garage. Just before she closed the door behind her, she turned around to stare at

Grandpa one last time; she didn't see the kind, loving grandfather that she loved anymore. That man was gone.

When the party ended, Ana searched for her sister. She found her in her bedroom reading a magazine. Ana wasn't sure if she should go in, so she lingered in the doorway, chewing on her lip.

Avery noticed but didn't look up. "Are you going to come in or just stand there?"

Ana took a deep breath and walked in, shutting the door behind her. "Avery, I need . . . I need to ask you something. It's about . . . Grandpa."

Avery's eyes remained steadily on the magazine, but her body tensed. Ana could see her grip tighten on the pages of the magazine.

"Did he ever take you to the garage?"

Avery looked up, her face red. "Sometimes. Why?"

"It's just . . ." Ana moved over to her sister's bed and sat down. She looked at Avery, unsure if she could even put into words what she wanted to say. She looked down at her hands and then back at her sister. "Never mind." She got up to leave.

"Ana, wait." Avery put her magazine down and turned her attention fully to her younger sister. "Did he touch you?"

"That's the thing. I don't remember, I only remember bits and pieces but it's like I blocked it out all these years and now I am starting to remember things, things I don't want to believe but that I know are true." Ana managed to say between soft sobs.

Avery looked down, tears spilling over her cheeks listening to her baby sister, realizing for the first time how bad this got for *her*.

"Maybe it's better, Ana, that you don't remember. Maybe you aren't meant to remember it all. Maybe your mind is trying to save you…because I didn't," she quietly chastised herself. Avery was pale and a little green, her hands shaking.

Ana watched her sister hang her head into her hands and then grow red around the ears. "Av-Avery are you okay?" Ana said as a whisper. She had never seen her sister turn this shade of red before. Avery stayed silent.

"Avery, I am so sorry, I should have just stayed quiet and kept playing pretend," Tears stung Ana's eyes; she hated seeing Avery this mad at her. Avery's head whipped up so fast it startled Ana.

"What did you just say?"

Ana gasped but she looked up at her big sister to answer. "I said, I am so sorry I said anything, you're so mad and it's all my fau–"

"STOP right there," Avery almost shouted and without waiting for her sister to respond, she reached out and grabbed her sister into a hug that came with such force, a force of pure protection. "Anastasia, it's me that is sorry. You were playing pretend, while I chatted away in the kitchen about meaningless things not realizing what was happening to you, my baby sister! I am not mad at you, I am furious with him, and if I am honest, with myself for not seeing this."

Ana let out a breath she didn't realize she'd been holding and for the first time in a long time, she felt safe in her sister's arms. Now they both knew and based on Avery's reaction, Ana knew things were going to start getting better.

Together, the girls stayed hugging and crying for what seemed like a very long time, and then Avery softly spoke the words Ana was dreading, "You need to tell Mom," Ana looked up at Avery with a scared look, "I'll be with you every step of the way and Ana, you will never have to play pretend again!" Avery such it with such conviction, Ana believed every single word.

* * *

The next day when Ana woke earlier than normal, she smiled as she found herself still wrapped in Avery's arms very protectively. She managed to untangle herself without waking her sister. She realized that because she'd told Avery, she wasn't really alone anymore. As she looked out of the open window to the horizon, she wasn't sure what to do next, but when she thought about this man—her grandpa, the one that told her amazing stories about life, the man who was supposed to teach her, the man that she could talk to for hours—she was only able to wonder how he could do these things to her, his Ana-cakes; her head became dizzy at the thought of the pain and betrayal.

She was so deep in thought, she didn't hear Avery wake. All of sudden she felt her sisters' arms wrap around her in a hug as she kissed the top of her head. Ana smiled and relaxed in her sister's embrace. They both enjoyed the morning breeze flowing through the room. With it came the most beautiful sunrise. They stood there watching the world awaken quietly together, knowing it was going to be a hard day.

It was Ana who first broke the silence, "How am I supposed to tell Mom that her dad, her hero, was really a monster?"

"I don't know but I need you to remember two very important things," Avery turned her sister around to face her. "One, Mom loves you very much and, two, this is NOT your fault."

Ana nodded and Avery held her hand out to her.

"Let's head downstairs, I think I smell mom's breakfast."

Ana looked down at her open hand and hesitantly took it, knowing that the next conversation was going to change her life and everyone she loved, forever.

Avery and Ana sat at the table while Sophia cleaned up the kitchen. The remnants of yesterday's party littered the house. The smell of fresh pancakes on the griddle filled the air. Sophia stopped tidying to check on the food, then prepared three plates and sat down with the girls. Like her sister, Ana kept her head low.

"Yesterday, you both acted like you were having the time of your lives," Sophia said, breaking the silence. "Today, you both seem upset. Talk to me, please. What's going on?" She looked back and forth between them, confusion furrowing her brow.

When neither girl spoke, Sophia said, "Ana, you were having so much fun yesterday with your cousins that you refused to let Shannon go home! It wasn't until we promised you'd see her in a few weeks at Thanksgiving that you let her go."

Ana raised her head and looked at Avery, who was staring at her with quiet encouragement, but still, Ana couldn't find the words that had to be said, they were ugly words, unbearable to even think when sitting face to face with her mother.

"Okay, family meeting," Sophia said, dropping her fork onto her plate with a loud clatter. Avery and Ana jumped. "What is going on with you two?"

Ana shook her head then looked her mom straight in her eyes. She took a deep breath. "Mom . . . don't be mad at me." Avery listened intently to see what she would say.

Sophia's face looked tight as if she was afraid of what Ana might say.

Ana picked at her lips, something she did when she was anxious about something. Sophia reached up a hand to stop her.

"My darling, I won't be mad. Just tell me what is going on, please," Sophia said.

"M-m-mom . . . I don't want to b-be around Grandpa anymore," she stammered, lowering her gaze to her plate.

Ana felt a wave of relief that she finally said something but didn't know where to look. Sophia watched her, patiently waiting for an explanation.

"He makes me feel uncomfortable, and well . . . I just don't really want to hang out with him anymore."

"Honey, this is Grandpa you're talking about," Sophia said, "and he loves you girls so much. What is really going on? Why do you feel that way, Ana?"

Avery finally looked up, tears forming in her eyes while she looked directly at her sister. "Ana, I think you need to tell mom the whole story."

Sophia looked at both of her girls. "I don't know what this is about, but I see you're hurting so much." Sophia got up and came to Ana's side. This was the moment of truth. Suddenly, Ana felt all her energy drain away, and she started shivering so violently that she collapsed to the floor and curled up in the fetal position.

In a single movement, Sophia and Avery were by Ana's side, exchanging looks of shock.

"Avery, what is going on? Why is she so scared? Tell me?" Sophia demanded, hurt and confused.

"Mom this is Ana's story and it needs to come from her, I'm so…" Avery was saying when Ana spoke up.

"I have something to tell you, and you are going to hate me!" Ana violently cried.

"I've never seen you like this before! Ana, my baby girl. You're scaring me. What's going on?"

"Mom, you're going to hate me. You are going to hate me!" Ana kept repeating it over and over.

"Never, my sweet girl!" Sophia said, gathering Ana up in her arms. Deep inside, Ana knew her mother understood that things would never be the same now.

In her mom's arms, everything started to fit like a puzzle. Ana realized she'd been haunted by the same dream for years now, and each time she never really knew who the man was that was in it, but now it was very clear, it was Grandpa who gave her bad thoughts and brought the darkness into her world. He made her feel cold, dirty, and alone. He made her feel ugly, and no matter how many times she scrubbed herself in the bath, no matter how many layers of clothes she wore, she could still feel his clutches burning her skin. No matter how many times she sneaked a spray or two of her mom's favorite perfume, she could still smell the oil and dirt of his hands; it would make her feel queasy. Ana instinctively knew this would be a smell that would forever haunt her. Six years ago, Grandpa had stopped wanting to play, stopped being lovable Grandpa, and worst of it all, he stopped being her best friend. Instead, he became the monster hiding in plain sight.

After every time, every painful moment, Ana's mind had blocked out the pain and filed it away. She'd put on an internal mask, one that hid the things he'd done. She couldn't get his voice out of her head, asking Shannon if she wanted to help him tinker. Once upon a time, those words had made her feel like the most special girl in the world.

Still in her mother's arms, it was as if time stood still and all of the memories flooded back, taking Ana by surprise. How could she have forgotten so many painful, horrific moments? How could her grandpa hurt her like that, hurt her body? He was supposed to love her and make her feel safe. He did the complete opposite, and no one noticed, because no one ever thinks the monster is someone you know, love, and trust. He stole her innocence, and her mind had hidden it from her. It was as if her mind was protecting her and hiding it from herself. Now that she knew, one thing was for sure, she had to tell her mom everything, just as she and Avery talked about. It was one thing being made to feel this way by Grandpa, but seeing him try and touch Avery that day she was helping with the light, then witnessing what happened between him, Shannon, and Lacey in the garage that day, who else could be in trouble? Who else could he hurt? Who else was he hurting?

She could hear her mom and Avery speaking to her, but the words were dulled compared to other noises. The humming of the extraction fan, the laughing of the children outside, a dog barking in the distance. Ana tried hard to focus, to silence her thoughts. She knew in her heart that she was about to do the most grown-up thing she'd ever done in her life.

"Mom . . ." she began to speak, raising her eyes slowly to look at her. "I need to tell you something . . ." Then it felt like the whole world just stopped.

Chapter 3

The tension in the room was palpable. No one dared to speak. Avery and Sophia watched her as they'd never watched her before. Things had changed forever. Ana took a deep breath and looked at her mother. A mixture of anxiety and fear filled her stomach; she could feel it gurgling. Ana was afraid she would throw up if she opened her mouth. The fear that her mother wouldn't believe her was paralyzing.

Be strong, Anastasia. Be brave. You need to speak up and tell Mom. You have to protect the family, she told herself. Avery's strength also helped her. She knew that once she spoke her truth, her life would never be the same. Whether it changed for better or for worse, only time would tell.

"Mom . . ." she said, swallowing hard. *How was she going to be able to say everything she wanted to say before she'd be crying too hard to speak?*

"Mom . . ." she said again, placing her hands under the table on her lap, pinching her legs to stop herself from crying. She needed to be strong. She needed to be clear, for the sake of her younger cousins and for the sake of any other kids.

"Mom . . . Grandpa hurt me," she finally blurted out, tears falling down her face. Ana felt herself quivering as if a cold breeze had come through the kitchen. She pinched herself again. Sophia looked at her but didn't respond right away. *Maybe she just didn't know what to say*, Ana thought. *Or maybe she was going to say Ana was lying. Or making things up.* Avery cleared her throat, to reassure her to continue.

"What do you mean he hurt you?" Sophia asked. Ana's lips trembled as tears stained her shirt. What she was about to say would change all their lives forever, and she knew it was her fault.

Would they believe her? What would this mean for her family now? Ana had never been more afraid. She wanted to run and hide. That was her new thing. When things got scary, she would take off and go.

Avery reached her hand across the table toward her. Ana kept hers under the table though. It was now clear that the pinching wasn't for stopping the tears; it was so she would feel pain—punishing herself for talking about something she shouldn't tell. She could feel the vomit coming up her throat. *Would Grandpa be mad? Had she betrayed him?* The thought came suddenly. *Who else would she hurt by talking about this, about him?* This was Grandpa; he was loved by everyone, including Ana, but . . . he betrayed her. *Or was it her fault? Did she ask for it?*

"Ana . . ." Sophia's voice cracked but was loud enough to jolt Ana from her thoughts. "Sweetie, what do you mean when you say he hurt you?" she asked, encouraging Ana to continue. "I need to know." To Ana, Mom's voice sounded broken already. *How could she tell her everything?*

And Avery's afraid, she realized. The lovely green of her eyes—the shade they'd both gotten from their father—were filled with pain and tears. *Was that the same pain she often saw in the mirror, only this time in her sister's eyes?*

Sophia's eyes were deep blue, the same color as Grandpa's. The same color eyes she had stared at, pleaded with; the same eyes she had once looked at with love but now only conveyed darkness and fear. Part of Ana was afraid she would see the same darkness in her mother's eyes. Her heart couldn't take it, so she kept her eyes down just in case.

"He does things to me . . ." Avery started to cry, but Ana's ears went numb; Ana needed to carry on. "I don't think he should be doing those things, but he does, and I can never stop him."

Sophia gasped but didn't interrupt.

"I asked him to stop, but he keeps hurting me, Mom . . ." Ana felt the weight on her chest get heavier. "And I know you'll be mad at me, but I promise I never asked him to do any of it. I asked him if we could just fix cars instead, but he wouldn't listen to anything when he got that weird look in his eyes and sound in his voice."

Sophia was white as a sheet, and Avery was crying softly. Still, she avoided their gaze, afraid of what else she might see. Ana was afraid her mother would be angry with her.

"I'm afraid of him. His hands hurt me. He touches me in places he shouldn't and makes me put my mouth…down there. He makes me do things that I don't want to, and I think he might try to do it to Shannon too—to any of the smaller kids," Ana broke off in a sob, which made Avery cry even louder.

"I don't want him to hurt them, Mom. Maybe you don't believe me, but I am really afraid that he'll hurt them too. I saw him in the garage with them, and he had that same *look* in his eyes; I know because he looks at me that same way sometimes. Mom, you have to believe me. You have to. I just can't take any more of this. I am so afraid, so scared." Ana finally let the tears flow. Her body shook. She put her hands upon the table to steady herself, afraid she might faint if she let go. She took in big, gulping breaths of air. Sophia sat in silence for a moment, tears falling as she moved swiftly to her daughter's side.

"My sweet, sweet Anastasia," she said, holding Ana and Avery's hands tightly in hers. Ana felt how tight her grip was, and even if Mom didn't believe her, she wasn't going to leave her to cry alone.

"My precious little daughter," her mother said between choked sobs. "Ana, darling, please listen carefully."

Ana looked up, afraid of what she might see. Sophia nodded, looking her straight in the eye.

"I believe you; I would never doubt you, ever. Please believe my every word because this is so important," she said. She gave Ana's hands a little shake. "None of this is your fault. I believe you, and I will make this right. I promise you."

Sophia looked at Avery, who was still sobbing softly. "You, too?"

Avery nodded slowly. "Not as bad as Ana, but yes. He's touched me. I'm so sorry, Ana. I should have said something sooner. It's my fault."

With that, Sophia got up and moved in between her two daughters. And just like they were two little babies, she swept them into her arms and hugged them tightly. "This is no one's fault. This stops now. Okay?" she said again. "We'll make this right, my darlings," she repeated, rocking both girls in her soothing embrace. "We'll make this right."

Ana snuck a peek up into her mom's eyes and to her relief, all she saw was pure, unwavering love and hurt for what *he'd* done.

* * *

The knock on the door was loud and urgent. Ana was startled awake. Looking at the clock, she saw it was 6:00 a.m. The sky outside was black, cloaking the house in complete darkness. After breakfast, Sophia had decided they all needed a Duvet Day to be together, much like when the girls were little and would get sick. It was a time to get in Mom's bed to watch TV and cuddle. It always made Ana feel better. She'd fallen asleep sometime during

The Lion King, and from the looks of her, so had Avery. Before she'd dozed off, she'd heard her mother speaking to her father on the phone. She was relieved she had adults on her side now: Dad, Mom, and Trisha. He'd be coming over after work to help make things better and even though Ana didn't quite know what that would mean, it sure made her feel better.

Ana felt her mother gently release her and get up to answer the door. She kissed them both, trying not to disturb them. But the knocking hadn't stopped, and Ana wasn't asleep anymore. She crept to the top of the stairs to hear what her mother would say.

Dad looked wet and worried when he came in. Her parents headed right into the kitchen. Ana followed, hoping to keep out of sight. The two of them having a meeting in private wasn't new. Sophia would often summon him last minute to discuss some kind of problem with the girls, but Ana knew he was not ready for this.

"I'm afraid this is going to turn your world upside down like it's done to mine and our daughter," Sophia said.

"That sounds pretty bad, Sophia," Robert said. "What is going on? You're worrying me."

"I hate to have to share such terrible information Robert, but . . ."

"Soph, what's going on?" Robert asked, the nerves in his voice giving him away. Ana heard her mother's voice catch in a sob. Peeking around the corner, Ana saw her father reach out his hand to his ex-wife. "Are the girls okay? Are you okay?" he asked, sounding desperate.

"The girls are fine right now," Sophia said, finally finding the strength to speak. "But I need to tell you something that's happened to our baby girl." Ana could hear the faint sobs coming from her mother. It made her feel so sad to see her family like this.

"What is it? What's going on?" Robert's voice became more serious, protective, and Sophia knew she had to say it. "Sophia, what happened to our daughter?"

Sophia took a deep breath and told him the events of breakfast. Taking breaks to release the sobs she had been trying to suppress, Sophia explained everything that Ana had said, including the fact that she felt at fault about it. Ana couldn't see his face, but she saw his fist as he clenched it and pounded the table. *Would Grandpa have reacted the same way if he got the same news about Mom?* Ana wondered. Yet here he was, the one causing all of this pain. *How could Grandpa do this to Mom?* Ana wondered for the first time. *To his daughter's daughter?*

Robert asked so many questions, and most of them, Sophia couldn't answer. Ana was tempted to go in and talk to her dad herself, but she held back. *Let the adults talk*, she thought, feeling the burden of her secret lift just a little more. Ana could sense her dad's protectiveness. He didn't even ask if there was a possibility that she was lying, which made Ana feel even better. It was clear she had her family on her side, and she wasn't going to be alone in this like she feared she could be.

"We have to support them both, but they will have different needs, of course, because Avery wasn't abused the same way . . . like Ana was," Sophia said. She fell to her knees and started crying with her hands cradling her face. Ana knew that her mother had been holding her emotions back from her, and now she saw pain, betrayal, and anger. When Sophia removed her hands from her face, Ana noticed a look she'd never seen before. Ana tried to get a better angle, but Sophia removed her hands from her face and stood up so fast that both Ana and Robert were taken aback.

And then she spoke, "Robert, that son of a bitch stole Ana's innocence for years—years, Robert—while I was right there . . ." Sophia walked around looking for something, and before Robert could ask, she started again.

"For years? Do you know what this is going to do to Ana?" Robert realized it was a rhetorical question, so he stayed silent until it suddenly become clear what she was looking for.

"Sophia, stop. Give me your car keys. You are not going over there tonight. You need to calm down before we approach him."

Sophia stared at Robert with determination until her shoulders dropped and she said, "I need a drink. Would you care to join me?"

"Sure, Soph. I'll stay awhile," Robert said, joining her at the table.

As Sophia looked at Robert, Ana noticed a glint in her eyes that she had never before seen. Before Ana had time to figure it out, her mother spoke, "That son of bitch put his hands on our baby girl, Robert."

"He stole her innocence, and we were in the next room. How did we miss this? I never suspected in a million years he would or could do anything like this, Robert, do you know how many times I asked her to go in the garage and tinker on the car or…"

"Sophia, enough. We could all say the same thing, question our every move, wondering why we didn't see it. This wasn't us. This was him." He got up and paced the kitchen. "Soph, the rage I feel right now . . ."

Sophia hugged him, and together, they cried. Ana was taken aback by their reactions, but she felt safer. She was happy both her parents believed her, but she also didn't want any of them doing anything stupid. When they both stopped crying, Sophia spoke up first, "The most important thing she needs from us throughout everything that's about to happen is that we believe her—without question!" And Robert agreed.

"Soph, I want to have more face time with the girls. I want—no, I need—them to feel protected," Robert said. Ana thought she heard a weird catch in his voice. "I need them to know their Dad will never let anyone hurt them . . . again." He burst into tears, and Ana gasped. This was the second time she saw her dad cry in her whole life, and both times were tonight.

"Robert," Sophia said, concern in her voice.

"My little girl has been violated, hurt, abused by her own grandfather, and I had no idea. How is it possible I didn't have a clue? How did I miss this?"

"We told them that family was their safe space," Sophia continued. "And for six years, she's kept this horrific secret. About my father!" Sophia was crying again, right alongside Robert. "Oh my God, Robert," Sophia blurted out suddenly. Robert looked at her with shock at her sudden outburst. "Remember when she was wearing all those layers of clothes? Oh my God, this is why; and to think I got mad at her over it! How could I miss that cry for help? I didn't even think this was possible. Robert, I promise I didn't know. I swear that every time . . ."

"Stop, Sophia! Of course, you didn't know. I would never think that of you. This is not your fault. Neither one of us are at fault. Please stop torturing yourself. Why would anyone suspect that your dad was molesting her? Don't blame yourself, please. You're a great mother!" Robert said with finality.

"I *know* you're right; but as her mom, I feel incredibly guilty for not seeing the signs, and I feel sick to my stomach for every time I asked her to join him in the garage to 'tinker' on the cars or the many other times I let them spend time together. They just seemed so close, I never imagined, Robert. I just feel like I'm grieving for her, like some part of her is gone forever and that bastard stole it from her—my own father!" Tears continued falling down her cheeks. Robert reached over to embrace her.

Together, they cried the loss of their daughter's stolen innocence.

"How can she ever forgive me?" Robert said. "How can I ever look at her in the eyes and tell her that I will always protect her?"

"Robert," Sophia said. "This isn't your fault either."

"But I've failed as a father."

"It's like you said: we didn't know," Sophia said.

No, thought Ana, from her vantage point where she was still perched on the stairs listening closely. *Neither of them knew of the darkness she faced at Grandpa's hands.*

"For now, we have to put our feelings aside and focus on Ana and her needs," Robert said. "Where is she?"

"We took a Duvet Day. I think she's still sleeping," Sophia answered. "Robert . . . I know what I have to do, and—before you say it—yes, I know it could tear the family apart, but there is no other way." They were in agreement: their little girl came first—no matter what.

* * *

Ana suddenly felt exhausted. She went back upstairs to lay down in her mother's bed, staring up at the ceiling while Avery slept next to her. Her emotional breakdown at breakfast had sapped her energy, and hearing her parents talk took the last bit of energy she had left. She didn't like to admit it, but she felt safer taking refuge in her mother's room. Ana thought back to the times when sleepovers in her mom's room were a regular occurrence when life was not so hard or painful. She was a little girl with big dreams. Ana let her tears fall. She couldn't help but allow a quiet sob to leave her lips.

"Ana?" Avery whispered out from the other side of the bed. "Are you awake?" She turned to face her sister.

"Yep." Ana turned over to face her sister nose to nose.

"You're so brave, you know," Avery said. Ana knew Avery wanted to comfort her.

"I don't feel like I am," Ana said, feeling guilty for everything.

"Well, you are. I wasn't able to do what you did."

Ana didn't reply. She felt heavy and numb at the same time. She wished she could make her sister happy by being grateful, but it was hard to pretend when she felt so overwhelmed.

"Ana, you told Mom about what was happening because you wanted to save our cousins. You're my hero, little sis." Avery smiled.

Ana had not thought of it that way. She hadn't felt like a hero at all. "I am?" she asked, confused.

"You are. You did a very brave and courageous thing, and all because you love our family. I'm so proud to be your big sister." Avery beamed at her. "If anything, I look up to you, my little sister."

"You do?" Ana asked, feeling somewhat uplifted at the thought she had made her sister proud. Avery had never said anything like that before, and it felt comforting to hear.

"Yes, I do. You're one strong girl. I'm so lucky to have you as my sister, so keep fighting, okay? Keep being you. Always know that from this day forward, I will protect you with my life." Avery leaned forward to kiss her little sister on the tip of her nose and hold her tight. With that, Ana closed her eyes and allowed herself to be cradled by her sister. Though her heart was heavy, she finally felt a tiny bit of hope.

* * *

It was late when Ana heard Robert talking to Trisha on the phone in the hall at the foot of the stairs.

"I know it's late," she heard him say. "But it'll be a while longer."

Ana wasn't sure she was ready to talk to her dad if that's what he had in mind. She curled up next to Avery who had already fallen back to sleep. Ana pretended to do the same. When Robert stepped into the room, she didn't move. She felt him standing by the bed watching them.

"I love you both so much," he whispered. "I failed you. I should have known something was wrong. I promise I will do better. I will protect you with all that I am. I will do better. I will be better."

Ana couldn't imagine her father being any more protective than he already was. Sophia's soft footsteps echoed in the hall. "You're going to drive yourself crazy. Come downstairs. We must do what we agreed we have to do."

Ana couldn't imagine what that was.

Sophia took a shaky breath. "I need to gather my composure," she said.

"We have to do this for our precious daughter. Ana was brave and selfless. We have to be too," Robert said. "I will be by your side throughout all of this."

They left the room. Ana, curious as ever, knew she needed to know what they were going to do next. She took her place outside the kitchen door, pressing herself against the wall of the hall to stay out of sight. Ana was shocked by what she heard. She expected Mom to call Grandpa and confront him. Or she thought Sophia would call Grandma and tell her about what has been happening. But she didn't call either of them.

"9-1-1? Yes . . . I'd like to report a crime."

* * *

It had been six months since Ana had told her family about the six years of abuse she had endured at the hands of Grandpa. Six months since her family had rallied around her, reminding her that she was brave and that they wholeheartedly believed her. Six months since her mother and father had called the police and had grandpa arrested and then released on bail. Six months in which Ana's life had completely changed. Brushing her blonde hair in the mirror, Ana couldn't help but notice the one thing that had not changed—her sadness. She couldn't remember the last time she felt any type of joy. She thought she would feel a lot lighter once her secret was out. Instead, the heaviness weighed her down more.

Ana relished the fact that she and her sister saw their father and Trisha a lot more now. In fact, tomorrow they would be going on a small trip together. Mom had been so busy with university deadlines that Ana was happy that Sophia would have a weekend to herself. Her aunt was coming over shortly too, which meant that her cousins Shannon and James would be over to play. It had been a while since she'd seen any of their family members, so it would be a nice, normal thing to do. Yet Ana didn't feel normal. She didn't feel happy or excited; she felt . . . empty. There would be periods when she would lose time in the middle of doing something, not remembering where she was or what was happening, like brushing her hair and not remembering picking up the brush.

Downstairs, she heard the doorbell ring, and Mom answered. "Ana! Can you come down here, please?"

Ana was greeted by her aunt in an overzealous way. It didn't feel genuine. It felt like she was putting on an act. Ana shrugged away her thoughts and smiled politely. Shannon was already in the living room coloring, James was sitting on the sofa next to Avery, both of them on their phones texting. Ana sat opposite Shannon on the floor and grabbed a coloring pencil.

"Hi, Ana!" Shannon beamed at her. It was clear the secret had not reached her yet. Maybe that was for the best. Ana smiled at her young cousin. James and Avery looked up for a brief second, smiled, and then carried on with what they were doing. It felt good for things to feel as normal as they could, and for once, it felt like it was going to be a good day.

A little while later, Ana watched her mother take Aunt Brooke into the kitchen, where they talked in hushed tones. Ana knew that soon enough the conversation was going to circle around to her, Grandpa, and the court case. Ana didn't want to listen. Mom would probably tell Aunt Brooke about the trip Dad was taking them on—just in time to avoid the court case. But Ana found her mind wandering to the conversation in the kitchen. She sidled over to the doorway to listen.

"Soph..." Brooke started. The sound of it made the hair on Ana's neck stand up. Lately, it felt like there was one piece of bad news after another. She'd have thought she'd be used to it at this point. But here it was. One hushed tone of voice and she was back on high alert.

"Oh, what is it?" Sophia sounded exasperated, nervous. Ana heard the bangles on her mother's wrist jingle. She always played with them when she was nervous.

"I've been talking to the others, and you know we stand behind you and Ana. We support you all." Aunt Brooke stopped and Ana couldn't imagine what was coming next.

"But, well, you see, Mom and Dad are getting older and . . . well . . ."

"Where is this going, Brooke? What about Mom and Dad?"

"The family still wants them to remain part of the family."

The words took her breath away. Ana felt like she had been punched in the stomach.

"I expected that," Sophia said. "I had hoped not to have to deal with that until justice was served and the court proceedings were done. I assumed that until then he wouldn't be at family functions." Sophia sounded more and more upset. "I thought when the judge locked him up this would take care of itself. I'm worried about how Ana will react."

"I'm sorry. It's not what you wanted to hear," Aunt Brooke said.

"I understand. It will be over soon anyway."

* * *

"Tag! You're it!" James patted Ana's shoulder and then ran away.

"Hey!" Ana giggled, looking to see where Avery and Shannon had run off to. Spotting Shannon hiding behind a tree, Ana started running in her direction. "Got you!" Ana shouted, grabbing hold of her cousin. Shannon screeched with laughter and tried to squirm away. As she freed herself, Ana's hand brushed against Shannon's chest. Suddenly, Ana stopped in her tracks with tears threatening to flow. Confused, James, Avery, and Shannon stopped running and looked at Ana. She ran into the house and straight to her mother.

Sophia took Ana to her room as she wailed. She let her daughter calm down before she tried to soothe her. "Honey, what's wrong?" Sophia asked, rubbing her back

"Mommy, I did something bad," Ana cried, her loud sobs deep and heavy.

"What did you do?" Sophia asked. "Last I saw, you kids were all playing tag and having fun."

"I touched Shannon here." Ana pointed to her chest.

Sophia looked stunned. "Ana, do you think you did something wrong?" Sophia rubbed Ana's back as she took big breaths in between her cries.

"It was an accident. You didn't do anything wrong. What happened to you might make that confusing for you."

"I have something inside."

Sophia's mouth was open a little, like she was shocked by Ana's admission.

"Ana! What do you mean? You're a good person!"

"It's like I can't move. I am scared I'm going to hurt someone. I get such bad feelings."

"The counselor called that 'the guilties,' remember?" Sophia said.

She looked up at her mother. That is what we all talked about. It made her feel a little less abnormal knowing it was a "thing."

"Ana, I worry about you. Please don't confuse what happened to you with touching other people. You can show love and affection," she said.

"But I could have hurt Shannon!"

"It's not the same as what you went through, darling. What grandpa did was on purpose, and he hurt you, knowing it was very wrong. You are doing nothing wrong. You were only playing with your cousins. Do you feel better now that you've told me?"

Ana thought back to the first meeting with her therapist when she explained what "the guilties" were and how it was normal for Ana to feel this way; she also told me it would get easier over time. "We want you to be a victor, not just a survivor," the therapist said. But she'd never used the word "abuse." Just hearing that word made her feel like a victim.

* * *

Trisha brushed Ana's hair as she dangled her feet into the cold river. It was the perfect sunny summer day, and she was grateful to have something cool to dip into. Avery was sitting beside her chatting about the hike they would go on later in the day, and Robert packed his fishing gear into the truck. They were up at the cabin, high up in the mountains. It was Robert's getaway, and Ana felt privileged whenever he shared it with them. Ana knew her mom needed time to catch up on her university work, but more importantly, she needed time to attend the hearing for Grandpa. Sophia had said she didn't want Ana to go through any more trauma so she didn't have to go.

"You look beautiful," Trisha said, giving Ana a hug. "Want me to do your hair next, Avery?"

"I think I'll go help Dad with the truck, but thanks," Avery said.

As Avery got up, she slipped. Ana gasped and reached out to keep her sister from falling in the river. As she did, her hand brushed against her bum.

Avery managed to stabilize herself. "Thanks," she said as she walked away.

Ana's hand burned. She stared at her fingers, blinking. *Were they becoming red?* Her ears heated up, and her chest felt heavy. Running to her father, she pinched herself to stop the tears from falling.

"Daddy . . ." she started, trying to catch her breath. In a hushed tone, she pulled him close.

"I touched Avery's bum. It was an accident; I swear." She felt apologetic and defensive at the same time. Robert stood up straight and looked at Ana.

"Ana, I've told you that you don't have to keep telling on yourself every time you touch someone." He sounded exasperated. This was probably the fifth time today that Ana had touched someone in what she deemed an inappropriate way, and each time, she confessed it to him.

"I know it scares you, but I don't know how to help you," he said. "Doesn't your counselor call it 'the guilties'?"

Ana nodded.

"She said you needed to work out your boundaries. We are all clearer about when we hug each other and stuff, right?"

Ana felt bad that everyone had to behave differently around her now. But she was so jumpy since her disclosure about Grandpa that she couldn't help it. She knew she was withdrawing from everyone, and she flinched when anyone touched her. She worried they were getting impatient with her, and Dad's tone didn't help reassure her.

"My happy-go-lucky girl, you're always so anxious and nervous now." Her Dad sounded so sad. His admission made Ana feel even more guilty.

"And I see you pinch yourself. Like you're punishing yourself."

"I'm sorry."

"No, don't apologize for that too! I hate to see how you've changed." Robert looked away and Ana felt guiltier than ever.

"Robert, this is new to all of us," Trisha said, coming up behind them. "Yes, Ana behaves a little differently now, but she's been through a lot."

"That doesn't stop me from feeling bad about it," he said.

Ana wrung her hands, the anxiety building up inside of her.

"You haven't done anything wrong. Let's get in the truck and go fishing," he said, holding the door for her. Ana got in, but something inside her knew today was not going to be the good day she had hoped for.

* * *

They had been fishing for a better part of the day, and aside from Avery dropping her rod into the water, their trip had been a success. Ana had even managed to catch a few small fish herself with some guidance from Trisha.

"We're going to be eating good tonight!" Trisha laughed as she looked into the cooler where they had been storing their catch.

Robert had caught some impressively sized bass, and Ana knew he was looking forward to the delicious meal Trisha was going to make out of them. He sipped on his beer and looked out over the amazing view. The sun was shining high in the British Columbia sky, the heat from the rays bouncing on the water. Ana tiptoed away. She waited until her father had closed his eyes for a moment. He looked so peaceful, enjoying the mountains and the fresh air the mountains provided. As quietly as she could, she lugged the cooler over to the side of the river. She cringed at the sound of thrashing in the water as she tipped the cooler full of fish into the river.

"Ana!" Robert shouted.

Ana looked in his direction. Avery looked up too, watching their dad running toward Ana. Trisha lifted her sunglasses off her face and got up from her chair. Robert grabbed Ana away from the water edge, and she dropped the cooler with a loud thud.

"Ana, why did you do that?" he shouted, his face red with anger. "We spent all day fishing and collecting food for dinner! All that hard work is now swimming free in the water!"

He grabbed Ana by her shoulders. Ana froze, her anxiety paralyzing her.

"Anastasia, why did you do that?" Spit came out from his mouth from sheer anger. Ana had never seen him so mad. *Why had she ruined such a perfectly good day?* Ana started to cry and ran over to Trisha.

"Calm down, Rob. She didn't mean to do it," Trisha tried to reason with him.

In a few short strides, he was back in front of Ana. "Why, Anastasia?"

"I'm sorry, Daddy," Ana stuttered.

"No, Ana. I asked you *why* you did that?" His angry tone rose again.

"Because the fish weren't happy being stuck in the cooler, Dad. They wanted to be free," Ana confessed.

Robert grabbed the can of beer in his pocket and threw it to the ground. It exploded from the impact, and beer sprayed all over Trisha and Ana. Robert got in the car, indicating it was time to leave. Trisha and Avery rushed to pack up as Ana sobbed silently. The family bundled into the car and drove back to the cabin in silence.

Chapter 4

Sophia arrived at the courtroom and sat out of sight from her father. From this viewpoint, she looked at the back of his head and saw him for what he finally was: evil. Her own mother was on her dad's side, and in that moment, she felt so betrayed seeing them both sitting near each other. *How could her own parents do this to her?* she thought to herself. She felt even more betrayed when she found out her mother had walked in on Ana and her father "playing pretend" and said nothing. That news had shocked Sophia to the core. *Her own mother!* She knew the growing headache was a sign of what she could expect the day to be like. *How could my own mother have seen THAT and just left poor Ana in his hands; she joined the party again like she saw nothing, how? How do people do this? I have to stop thinking like this, or I won't make it through the proceedings.*

With that thought, she tried to calm herself down. Brooke was beside her, a true friend and sister. Since this all had unraveled, it felt very much like, while her family believed and supported Ana, there was much more public acceptance for her father than she expected. *How could that be?* she thought to herself. *He hurt my baby for years and essentially stole her childhood!* The more she thought about it, the angrier she got. *Today is the day I've been waiting for. Today I finally get to see my father punished for all that he had done to my little girl*, she thought, both angry at him and herself for not seeing it.

The worry of bumping into him at the shops would no longer be a problem nor would she have to worry about seeing his face at family gatherings. Ana would be free to be a kid again, and she would no longer have to hold her breath every time there was a chance her daughter and father could accidentally cross paths. She had been praying, hoping, and wishing that she could witness justice. While she loved her father, she hated him too. Once he was served his punishment, she could finally stop feeling guilty for the internal conflict she had and, instead, work on improving the lives of her daughters.

The judge had been talking for a while, but she couldn't listen. All she was waiting for was the sentencing; hearing all the details again was unbearable. For one moment, she allowed herself to drift into a daydream of welcoming Avery and Ana back from their trip and telling them the good news: That Grandpa was in prison and would no longer be able to hurt anyone again.

The gavel pounded on the table, and Sophia's mother began to wail. She'd missed the moment the verdict was called out. Panicked, she looked around the room. Brooke held her hand. They looked at each other. Tears welled up in her sister's eyes. "I'm sorry, Soph." Brooke cried, hugging her tightly.

"Wait . . . what?" I asked, looking around her. People were getting up from their seats; her parents were embracing. *What is going on? Was it over?* "What happened?" Sophia asked Brooke, pulling her away from everyone.

"He's gotten away with it," Brooke said, solemnly looking at their dad, or evil incarnate as Robert would have said.

Sophia was approached by her lawyers wanting to speak to her, but her vision went blurry. Their voices echoed as if they were far away.

He had been found guilty, one victory in a sea of disappointments. He had to register as a sex offender, do community service, and would have to attend Alcoholics Anonymous. Apart from that, he would be allowed back into the world. He would still be at family functions, and worst of all, there was no true punishment for what he did. He could walk free and no one would know the evil he harbored inside of himself or how he had allowed it to destroy his own family, his own granddaughter. Sophia began to cry. Justice was not served today. She felt the system had failed them. She allowed herself to once again be hugged by Brooke, letting herself fall into her sister's arms as she lost the ability to carry herself.

How would she explain this to the girls? How could she tell them that when someone does something bad, they would be punished when their own grandfather was let free after doing what he did to them? Not only had they been failed by the courts, but she had also failed Ana. How would she be able to feel safe now? Ana was already struggling with relationships within her family; Ana was a very strong girl but she knew her daughter was close to her breaking point and this. . .this ugly, joke of a verdict was not going to help.

She felt like she'd let her daughter down again. Tears welled in Sophia's eyes as she lay awake that night in the quiet of her bedroom. She was grateful at least that Ana wasn't there, and she was having fun with Robert and Trisha. That was the only silver lining she could come up with, but she drifted off to sleep wishing she could hold her baby girl and make everything okay again.

* * *

Robert dropped Trish and the girls at the cabin and immediately took off for a hike. Ana saw tears in his eyes as he stormed off to climb a mountain and clear his head. Trish joined her at the window to watch him go. Before he got out of sight, they both gasped when they saw him punch a tree, then clutch his hand into his chest. He'd looked up at the sky and seemed to howl something, but they couldn't make out what. Only the sound of his anger and frustration was clear.

"Why would he do that?" Ana asked Trish, hours later.

"He's hurting for you. He sees life is hard for you now, and he wants to fix it. But he knows he can't."

"He's been gone for hours," Avery said quietly so Trisha wouldn't hear sitting by the open windows watching as the sun went down. The place felt eerily quiet but she didn't say anything.

"The sun is setting in the distance, and it's already getting chilly," Ana said. "I'm worried."

"Me too. How far do you think he hiked?"

Ana shrugged. She imagined him standing on the mountain looking down at their cabin. He felt very far away.

"Is this what life is going to be like now?" Ana asked.

"What do you mean?" Avery turned to face her sister.

"Is this the new normal everyone is talking about?"

"Ana," Avery said with a warning sound in her voice. "Don't go there."

"What if nothing is ever the same?"

That's the problem, Ana thought. *The real problem is that I'm broken, and he can't fix me. No one can.* She'd heard her parents call her "fragile" behind her back. She knew they focused on her and not her sister. She saw Avery pulling away and growing up more and more on her own. It was all her fault.

* * *

How am I supposed to be her parent? Robert thought to himself as he surveyed the landscape around him. *She flinches when I hug her, and it only reminds me of the biggest failure of my life. I can't physically comfort and hug my own daughter because of that son of a bitch!*

Trisha was in their marriage by herself because Robert was spiraling into depression, a secret he felt he needed to keep from her. On more than one occasion, he had found himself stepping into traffic hoping there was an easy way out he could take. Robert was exhausted: mentally and physically. His heart hurt for his baby girl and for the life she would no longer have, the innocence and the joy of discovering life for herself. Then there was the part of him that was scared for her future if she ever decided to have children. Would she be afraid to let him love them? Would he be punished for something he didn't do? Would he lose the ability to have a strong relationship with his daughter because he was a man? Robert couldn't stop the thoughts, and he found his mood darkening even more. There was no hope, no point, no escape. Except . . .

He took a step closer to the edge of the cliff. The view was phenomenal from where he stood, and yet, he couldn't allow himself to enjoy it. It all felt so meaningless when despite the beauty of the world, there was still so much pain. He wanted to take it away from his daughters, but he couldn't as he didn't know how. One thing he did know was how to take it away from himself, *at least then Ana wouldn't have to worry about him anymore.* Another step closer to the edge, past the safety railing now, he was so close he could feel the air from below trying to push him back to safety. It would only take one more step for him to make it all go away. His girls would be much better off without him, then he couldn't fail them anymore. He would not be a threat to their happiness. He could just make it all go away.

Robert felt faint. He was close to the edge, and still, he was holding on to the railing. His mind wanted him to let go, but his heart kept him grounded. The tears flowed heavily. His mind was screaming at him, and yet, he couldn't take his hands away from the only thing keeping him safe. A gust of cold wind blew into his face, waking him up from the deliriousness he was feeling. Like a jolt of energy, Robert wiped his tears, steadying himself once again and climbing back over the railing to a safe distance from the edge.

He shook his head to clear his mind and began walking down the mountain. Ana and Avery were incredibly brave. They were handling everything much better than the adults seemed to be. While everything felt incredibly unclear and frightening, they continued to take every day as it came. Sure, Robert was their father, but he didn't need to know everything. Then the realization suddenly hit him: the only time he truly failed them was when he stopped trying. He picked up his steps. He was far from okay, far from clearing the pain and darkness he was clouded by, but right now, his girls needed him, and it was not such a bad thing that he needed them too.

* * *

Sophia typed furiously on the keyboard. She had been in the university library for hours, having used it as an escape to get out of the house. She had a paper due in the next few weeks. Trying to get work done at home was not helping her. She didn't want to be home alone in the silence. So, after fighting procrastination for hours, she found herself driving to a place where she could find solace, and that was the campus library.

Her mind kept wandering back to a few days ago when she watched as her family was denied justice for the awful things her father did. She saw her mom and dad cry with happiness as her hopes of retribution for Ana's pain were taken away, and their lives as they knew it continued to change.

Sophia felt selfish for wanting to focus on her studies. As a single mom who worked a full-time job, she was told, by her mother and many other people who were meant to support her, that going back to university was a foolish dream. It was her girls who gave her the courage to go for it anyway. Life seemed much simpler then than it did now. Time was a funny thing and so much could happen in a blink of an eye.

    She kept typing away, determined to make a dent on her assignment. She was not going to leave the library until she finished her work or was hungry. She was hoping the former would come first. Yet every time she started making headway, she would find herself thinking about how Ana was going to cope with life going forward, how Avery would be affected by the things happening with the family. Something their family therapist kept warning her about stuck in her mind, "Children of sexual abuse will likely act out promiscuously in their teens." Was that what her daughter was in for? Was that another by-product of what her father caused? Sophia reflected on all of the pain Ana was now inevitably going to go through, all because she missed the signs. *What signs?* she couldn't help but ask herself. *Was I supposed to question the bond my children had within our happy family?* All too painfully, she now understood. Yes. Yes, she was. She learned the hard way that anything was possible, and people were not always what they seemed to be . . . *but her own father?* She rested her head on her books and broke out into tears. How could her own father do this to her? To her daughter? Life was never going to be the same for her energetic, loveable, and fearless daughter, and there wasn't much she could do about it.

    After what felt like hours of crying, she finally lifted her head and looked at her computer in front of her. Being the resourceful and strong woman she was, Sophia looked on her search engine for answers. After typing out several search terms, she had started to feel like knowing what to expect would help her be a better support system for her daughters and perhaps even make her a better-equipped parent. She was shocked to learn that most child sex abuse happened with someone they knew and trusted; that alone made her nauseous. It made her feel sick to see the number of pages dedicated to providing support for children affected by abuse, particularly sexual abuse. Sure, there was comfort in knowing there were resources available to her, but it made her feel ill that there was even a need for such literature. Should she have been comforted by the thought that other parents were dealing with the same things? Or completely broken and saddened by the fact that there were many more kids like Ana?

Sophia read quietly to herself, trying to absorb the information she was reading. "Children who suffer from sexual abuse can be prone to self-destructive behavior . . ." She carried on reading, getting lost in the knowledge of the topic and how much she needed to look out for, and yet, there was so little on how she needed to support her daughter without being so intrusive. Sophia sighed and rested her head back on the desk. Studying for a psychology degree seemed so exciting before. Now she felt like she was living the studies she read in textbooks. *None of this is easy*, she thought to herself, feeling like the weight of the world was on her shoulders.

Still, there was hope that Ana could be fine. Avery may come out of this undamaged, but for the first time in her life, Sophia dreaded the coming days, even the coming years. She was not ready to see the aftermath of her father's betrayal.

No amount of research or case studies could prepare her for the challenges they had yet to face, because after all, there was no real guide on how to move forward positively when you've been betrayed by someone who was once your hero, who *was your father*.

Chapter 5

Ana pushed her long blonde hair out of her face as she swayed to the music. She had her party mask on. He took a small white pill out from his pocket and held her face delicately. Her mouth opened, allowing him to slip the pill discreetly through her lips. Within seconds, she felt elation, her heartbeat quickening and the music deafening. With his arms draped around her, she felt protected.

Ana danced away the feeling of insecurity. She belonged to that club, and she knew it. The eyes of jealous girls and admiring men fixed on her. She loved the attention and even more so loved the idea that she was untouchable in the sea of people. Her beauty radiated confidence and class, but only she knew the truth. Here, she felt like she could be anybody and be anything.

She looked at Carter dancing; she felt his body and the warmth it exuded. She knew he was bad for her, but she couldn't resist him. She was like a moth to his flame. At some point, she would get burned. Until that happened, she would keep going back to him. Carter kissed her cheek, the smell of alcohol and cigarettes on his breath. She didn't care. His attention was on her, and that was all that mattered.

From behind her came a tug. Trying to shout above the music, Ana's friend, Haven, called for her to come outside. Too drunk and high to object, Ana willingly followed her friend to the smoking area outside the club.

Haven lit up a cigarette and Ana lit up her joint. "Ugh, Anastasia!" Haven called out, making a face. "That stuff stinks!" she said, pushing Ana's rolled concoction away from her. Ana laughed and took another drag. She closed her eyes and waited for the hit to make her feel good. The smell attracted a guy to her left. As he approached the ladies, he made small talk as he pulled out his own poison of choice. The girls stayed and chatted as his friends joined in the conversation. Soon enough, Haven was talking to a group of men as Ana was making out with the one who originally approached them. Groping her body, Ana unashamedly relished in the attention. She let his hands explore her as she let hers feel his muscular body.

 From behind her, she could hear Carter's voice. He had managed to find them and was more annoyed that she was indulging in drug-taking without him than the fact that another guy was groping his girl. Riding on his high, he lit up his wacky cigarette before putting his arm around Haven. Finally, Ana pulled herself away from her new friend and winked at Carter. He laughed and pulled her beside him. "You've had your fun!" he said to the stranger. "Now it's my turn." As he twirled Ana around him and slapped her ass, Ana giggled and took a puff from his cigarette. One more shot, one more hit, one more dance. It was late, but Ana most definitely didn't want the night to end.

 She had grown to find true peace amidst the chaos of the club scene. She had made so many friends and had been exposed to so much of the "real life" that school felt meaningless. Haven was her best friend and was just as wild as she was. Not to mention she was not judgmental and always willing to experiment. It was crazy to think that here, in this club, surrounded by sex, drugs, and alcohol, she felt much safer than at home.

Haven pulled Ana again. "We've got to go!" Haven shouted, still straining to be heard above the thumping music.

Ana looked at her pleadingly. "Come on! Five more minutes!"

Haven sighed. She knew what that meant. Five more minutes often led to them getting home in the early hours of the morning, which was never a problem as her mother often worked night shifts in the hospital where she worked as an ER nurse. "Not tonight, Ana." Haven shook her head. They had a practice exam in science class the next morning, and while both were incredibly intelligent, they were not doing too well that semester. They said their goodbyes, exchanged numbers with their new friends, left Carter with them, and got into the taxi.

Ana laughed as she settled into her seat, reveling in what a great night they had. As they made their way back to Haven's house, Ana closed her eyes and put her head against the window. She breathed a sigh of relief at the touch of the cool glass against her warm forehead. Haven was chatting animatedly about the events of the evening as Ana grunted every so often to show she was listening. She found herself starting to drift off, then quite suddenly, they were piling out of the car and getting straight into Haven's bed. Ana found herself spinning as the drink and drugs began to catch up with her. She closed her eyes once again, hoping that she wouldn't feel it in the morning. Soon enough, she was sound asleep with her ears still ringing and her heart still thumping from the night's activities.

* * *

As soon as Ana got through the front door, she could smell the omelets. While she was usually a huge fan of her mom's cooking, last night's alcohol and lack of food were still wreaking havoc with her stomach, and Ana feared she would throw up. Trying to sneak upstairs, her mother came around the corner and both were as surprised as the other.

"Hi, darling!" Sophia said in her usual musical way. Ever since Avery had come home for college break, her mother had been in much higher spirits, and it was starting to annoy Ana. "How was school?" she asked, trying to start a conversation. Ana knew she would not be able to get to her bed and take a quick nap before her shift at the diner, so she just followed her mom into the kitchen.

"It was fine," Ana mumbled, trying to make it clear she was not up for a conversation, but Sophia was not willing to have the usual short one-sided chats she had with her youngest daughter. She was way too happy to let Ana's bad temper spoil her last day with Avery.

Avery came down to the kitchen, her long blonde hair and boho style captivating the room. She was beautiful, growing up to be the smart and caring girl Sophia had always hoped her to be. Avery was a twenty-year-old, soon-to-be, University of British Columbia graduate who had worked extremely hard to be the upstanding young woman she was. Sophia sighed as she looked at Ana slumped across the table trying to stay awake. Her beautiful sixteen-year-old had seemed to be a little lost nowadays. Since Avery left for the campus life at Kelowna for UBC, Ana had become more withdrawn. Sure, they were still close as far as mothers and daughters could be, but she knew in her heart Ana was doing her very best to pull away. That is why Sophia was so happy whenever Avery came home. Her older daughter brought with her some familiarity and would often be successful in bringing out bits of the old Ana that Sophia missed so much.

"It's a shame we missed you last night, Anastasia," Sophia said, nudging her daughter awake.

"Yea . . . sorry, I had a study session at Haven's," she mumbled, grabbing a piece of omelet and putting it on her plate.

"Maybe we could have dinner tonight?" Avery asked hopefully to her younger sister. Ana did not respond and instead carried on eating.

"Ana, what do you think? It'd be nice to hang out before I go back," Avery said again, looking at Ana and waiting for her to reply.

"I can't. I've got work in a few hours," Ana said. Looking up at Avery, she saw the hurt in her sister's eyes, and a guilty feeling made her stomach turn. "But maybe we could have breakfast at the café tomorrow before you go?" she asked, bringing a smile to Avery's face.

"Sure thing!" Avery responded before happily helping herself to more of her mom's cooking.

Shortly after breakfast, Ana excused herself to get ready for work. Feeling refreshed after her shower, Ana browsed on her phone and responded to texts she had received that day. Haven had left her a few messages letting her know how her practice test had gone. Ana had, of course, aced it and so did Haven.

She had messages from Carter telling her about some new weed he had managed to get for them to try. Then she saw a message from the mystery guy she met last night, asking her if she and Haven wanted to go to this new club across town. Ana sighed. If she didn't have to work late, she would go. But also, she could hardly turn up to breakfast with Avery hungover. She didn't want her sister to know about her secret life. Ana decided not to respond. She lived by the philosophy "never say never."

* * *

Ana cleared the table, huffing at the mess left by the family previously occupying the diner's table. Even though she was a wayward teen—as her mother had described her—she still respected others enough to leave a table in a tidy order for the poor servers having to do the dirty work. Perhaps it was her experience working in a diner. Or maybe it was her mother's insistence to always treat everyone with respect, but she made a policy of clearing whatever mess she had made before leaving a place. Considering the number of times she'd willingly cleaned up Carter's mess after one of their binges, it did not seem fair for minimum wage staff to have to deal with that.

Leaving the table sparkling clean, Ana turned to see an elderly lady sitting alone in the corner of the diner. She had seen her there almost every day for the past two weeks, and each time, Ana was her server. She always ordered the same thing: boiled eggs and toast with a glass of tap water. A tip of $10 was always left, no matter what condition the food came in. *She must be lonely*, Ana thought to herself. Why else would she spend two hours every day in this rundown diner, slowly eating her meal and jumping at every opportunity to chat with anyone? The lady tried hard to speak to Ana. The most Ana had ever spoken to her was to take her order, even though she had memorized it by now, and then to say goodbye when the lady left. While Ana had never formally introduced herself, the lady had always called her Anastasia, something she no doubt knew of because of her name tag. Sometimes Ana felt guilty for never asking for her name. Shaking off her thoughts, Ana picked up her cleaning tray and went out back to have a smoke.

Inhaling in and out, Ana couldn't help but dream for her life to be different. Despite only being sixteen years old, she felt like she had been stuck in Maple Ridge forever. She sometimes wished she was from Vancouver, the big city with the action, lights, and concerts, instead of their small town with a mere population of just over eighty-two thousand; she dreamed often of living in a bigger city with the glamour, flash, the rich, and the famous. But no. Here she was working in a small family-owned diner. She had barely even explored anything outside her town lines, with the exception of her frequent visits into the heart of Vancouver to get a taste of the nightlife.

There was so much more of the world she wanted to see, and yet, there was never any time. Between trying to finish school, her active secret life, and work, Ana felt like every single day seemed to be the same. That is probably why she had been living such a busy nightlife, which mostly consisted of meeting people from outside of the city who had no clue who she was. At night, she pretended to be who she wanted to be: a confident, self-assured woman. She got a thrill from fooling people into thinking she was older than she was, like she belonged in the masses of businesspeople looking important in the city. Sure, the heels hurt her feet, but she liked the sense of belonging, even if it was just for a night. It made her feel powerful, and it was in those times she felt like a stronger version of herself. She thrived in the adventure of using her fake ID, her body, and her looks to get anything she wanted. She knew the men were only interested in one thing, and she was happy to oblige. Ana loved getting all dressed up to allow the men to ogle her. Ana enjoyed the alter ego she had created for herself. This mask of the beautiful and untouchable is exactly what she wished meek little Anastasia could be. While Anastasia wanted to blend in the background and be unrecognized among the crowd, Ana grabbed at every opportunity for attention. It made her feel more confident, sexy, and stronger. But that was only at night.

Ana begrudgingly walked back into the diner, scanning the area. She noticed a lack of foot traffic today. Feeling optimistic, she hoped she would be sent home early, which meant she could go out after all. But first, she would need to wrangle Haven in on the plans. That way, she could use a sleepover as an excuse to not go home. Ana excitedly texted Haven, waiting for a response, which in typical Haven fashion came seconds later. Three simple words glowed on her screen: *Let's do it!* Ana beamed at her phone. She loved the fact that Haven, who also came from a single-parent household, was alone a lot. Though if you looked at the situation for what it was, it was actually quite sad. Haven's mom worked hard, that was for sure, but that didn't mean she worked extra hard to be a good mom. Ana and Haven had been friends since they were thirteen and had met in high school. Both broken and feeling incredibly alone, they had formed a close bond over their dislike of family life. Haven had no idea of the trauma Ana had been through, but that was just fine because Haven had her own too. They both knew there were secrets they were keeping from each other, and sometimes Ana wondered if they were more alike than they realized. But still, neither ever acknowledged it, and when together, they did their best to keep each other from spiraling into the darkness that often haunted them both.

Ana looked up and saw that the old lady was still sitting there, looking at the clock. It read 7:30 p.m. She should have left thirty minutes ago, and yet, she was still sitting there staring out at the window. Ana was not sure what prompted her to approach the lady, but there she was, not minding her own business, walking toward her.

"Hello, ma'am," Ana said, putting on her fake service worker smile. "Can I get you anything?" she asked, making her smile wider.

The lady looked up and smiled back. "Hello, Anastasia. How has work been?" she asked, politely motioning for Ana to sit opposite her. Automatically, Ana, or the Anastasia part of her persona, did as she was told and sat down.

"Work? It's been okay. Quiet, I suppose," Ana replied. "Can I get you anything?" she asked again.

The lady continued to ignore her question, seeming to be deep in thought.

"Are you okay?" Ana asked gently, pinching herself under the table, knowing that no good ever came from sticking your nose in other people's business.

"I'm fine, dear. Thank you," the lady replied, smiling again "I'm just having one of those funny days," she added, sighing and looking back out at the window again.

"Is there anything I can help you with?" Ana asked, once again punishing herself for continuing to chat with this stranger, but frankly, it was much better than pretending to work.

"That's nice of you. Thank you, but no. Just a chat is plenty for me," she said, not taking her eyes away from the window.

"Are you lonely?" Ana finally blurted out, unable to stop herself from asking the one question she had been thinking about since they first met. This made the lady snap out of her thoughts and look at Ana again, her smile still on her face.

She thought for a moment and then replied, "Yes, I suppose I am. Are you?"

Equally caught off guard by the question, Ana also took a moment to think before replying, "Yes." Tears welled up in her eyes. She pinched herself again under the table. Ana had not cried in years and had no idea what her emotions were doing at that very moment.

"That's probably why we've met then," the old lady said, simply smiling again. Ana smiled but she felt unnerved. She had buried emotional Ana for so long that it felt strange to be this vulnerable with a stranger. She stayed sitting for a while as they talked about things that truly had no meaning, like how the weather was, whether the mall was going to be built before Christmas, and what the lady was going to do that weekend. Weirdly enough, Ana felt comforted by talking to this stranger. It was like old Ana was finding a friend, even if old Ana did not exist anymore. The lady talked about her previous life and how she had spent all her youth chasing her dreams.

"Did you achieve your dream?" Ana asked excitedly.

The lady nodded.

"But what was the dream?" Ana asked again, like a little kid desperate for more information.

The lady looked outside the window. "I wanted to rule a male-dominated world," she said softly. "Run my own publishing company, and I did just that. Made my fortune and lived my life."

"And then what?" Ana inquired, feeling the warmth of excitement in her chest.

"And then I fell in love and went to chase that dream too," the lady replied with a clear shine in her eyes, reflecting on the memories flashing back to her.

Ana looked away. She did not want to see the lady cry. "Do you regret falling in love?" Ana asked.

The lady shook her head. "No, my dear. It took me on a new adventure. Andrew was the love of my life, and he loved me, even when I put work first." She looked around at the diner. "This was our favorite place to eat."

Ana laughed, also looking around. "This dump?" She could not help but find the idea of two high-flying businesspeople coming here to eat crazy.

"Oh, it was much nicer back in my day. It was our place to go where we didn't have to wear suits and could be whoever we wanted to be, eating our key lime pie and laughing the day away."

Ana thought for a moment about how strange it was that in such an ordinary place, two people could be whoever they wanted to be. For Ana, it was a prison cell that paid her. They talked more about the lady's career and how she worked up the corporate ladder and became a force to be reckoned with. Ana could not help but to marvel at this frail lady ruling with an iron fist in a world dominated by old, white men. Yet here she was: an ordinary-looking lady reminiscing on the good old days in the greasy spoon Ana called work.

"So why doesn't Andrew come here with you?" Ana asked, feeling a little sheepish at her intrusive question.

"He passed away a long time ago dear. In fact, today is the anniversary of his death." The lady sighed and stared at her hands. Ana heard the sadness in her voice and pinched herself again. It had been a long time since she had felt this connection with anyone and so came the guilt of seeing someone in pain.

After a few more minutes, the lady got up to leave. Ana said her goodbyes. Then, as the lady went to walk out of the door, Ana called out to her, "Wait . . . I'm sorry, but I don't know your name."

"Call me Grace, my dear." Grace smiled at Ana softly. With that, she walked out the door, leaving Ana with only the sound of the chimes that rang every time someone walked in and out of the diner.

* * *

Ana pushed the mystery guy up against the wall of the toilet cubicle and started unbuttoning his pants. He groaned as she touched him ever so softly on the back of his neck with her other hand. It was barely 10:00 p.m. and she was already so drunk that she had forgotten the guy's name. She had sheepishly admitted to herself that he was listed as "mystery guy" on her phone and had told her his name a few times already. *Was it Gary? Or Barry?* He lifted her up as she wrapped her legs around his waist.

Quietly, she moaned, "Oh Larry!"

He laughed. Pulling her away from him, he looked into her eyes. "Babe, my name's Harry. Remember?"

Ana rolled her eyes, pulled him closer to her again, and eagerly kissed him.

Haven swirled her cocktail as she tried not to look bored by being chatted up by some drunk businessman. Friday nights in the city were all the same, no matter what club you went to. Pent-up, angry, male egos walked around determined to feel more manly, and she did not even mind because it meant she could drink for free all night. Looking across the club, she scanned the crowd for Ana. She had been gone for half an hour now, disappearing with a random guy from the other night. Knowing Ana, she knew not to be worried. But she did not enjoy being left to fend off the hungry vultures. From the other side of the room, Ana appeared, her blonde hair illuminated by the club lights. Her perfect smile headed straight in Haven's direction. Breathing a sigh of relief, Haven grabbed her handbag, made up a lame excuse, and left the uptight accountant at the bar.

"Where have you been?" Haven shouted, pulling Ana away from Harry.

Ana asked for him to get them drinks, and like a lovestruck puppy, he obediently did so.

Haven laughed. "What do you do to these men?"

Ana smiled coyly and pulled out some pills from her bag. Handing one over to Haven, they raised their glasses, put the pill in their mouths, and took a drink.

Dancing the night away, Ana and Haven, like two little girls, had spent a good amount of time running away from Harry. Only joining him every so often to get free drinks, they had decided that tonight was going to be a girl's night. The girls made new friends as they drunkenly took selfies while dancing on the bar top. All the men watched and cheered them on. That night, Ana had her long blonde hair in soft, long, big curls. Her bright green eyes were accentuated by her makeup, and she wore a gorgeous tight, short black dress accessorized with lots of diamonds. It was easy to see why all eyes were on her. She exuded confidence and sex appeal.

Dancing slow and seductive to the music and moving her hips in all the right ways, she caught the attention of a tall, dark, handsome man across the room wearing a very expensive suit. He looked like someone who knew what he wanted and got it when he wanted it. She caught him staring and looked away, but it was too late. He caught her returning his look. Ana liked it when she had the upper hand in the bar. This alluring stranger seemed like the shy type, but she knew he was interested. Now he had her attention and he knew she wanted him. Ana gestured to the men down below her, and they gladly helped her down from the bar. She slowly and seductively danced her way over to him, moving her body to music. He could not take his eyes off her: how she swayed her hips, the way her hands roamed over her body. She knew he could see her desire and lust for him. In his eyes, she could see how much he wanted her, but his nerve got the best of him. *Was he really that timid, or would he be the type to change as soon as they left the bar?* The thought left her mind as quickly as it came because if she was honest with herself, she didn't really care anymore; she was running the show.

    Ana made her way through the crowd until she finally approached him. They were so close she could smell his expensive cologne, and it only made her want him more. As an adult, she preferred being the lion, since she spent her childhood being the lamb. They were so close, she felt his lips near her ear. She whispered to him and asked his name.

    "I'm Josh," he introduced himself, shouting over the music.

    She turned around, giving her back to him while she ground against him, allowing her hands to wander all over him as she swayed her body tight against his. She could feel that he wanted her. When Anastasia was at the clubs, she was in control. All she needed was the right sexy outfit, confident smile, makeup, and seductive moves. Ana learned men were not very complicated.

Turning to face him, she asked, "You're a good boy. Aren't you, Josh?" she asked, making her voice sound smooth and silky, still grinding her body against his. Ana loved to dance; it was the one outlet that made her feel in control and free. It was hot in the bar and her black dress didn't leave much to the imagination, but he tried to look when she wouldn't notice. Ana smirked. She knew he was looking.

"What naughty things can I make you do, Joshua?" she asked, knowing she was going to get exactly what she wanted. His eyes widened, but his smile never left his face as Ana roamed his body with her hands, rubbing over his taut abs. She pulled him closer and pressed her lips against his. One of his hands was around her waist; she guided his other hand up her skirt so he could feel just how much her body wanted him.

"Take me back to your place, and I'll see if you're a good boy after all." With that, Ana let Josh lead her out of the club.

* * *

Ana knew she had made a big mistake. She always felt like she was fighting herself to not be a terrible influence on other people. She pulled out her journal and started putting down everything she could think of. Her guilt from last night with Josh filled several pages. Writing made her feel like her situation was better, even though it wasn't.

The next morning, she found her way back to Haven's after her night with Josh. She had coaxed him into having his first taste of drugs, and they had spent the whole evening and the early hours of the morning drinking and having sex. Haven had also found herself a nighttime companion and had only made it home ten minutes before Ana did. While Ana changed for her breakfast date with Avery, she and Haven caught up with each other on the events of the previous night. Ana shared her guilt of introducing innocent Josh to ecstasy. Haven assured her that he was a willing participant and was not forced in any way. Ana agreed with her despite the deep feeling of doubt inside her. Truth be told, she still felt very intoxicated, but hopefully not enough to be too obvious.

 Saying goodbye to Haven, Ana spritzed herself with perfume and dashed out of the door. Hopefully, Avery wouldn't notice.

Chapter 6

Avery sipped on her coffee as she looked at her watch. Ana was late but she was hardly surprised. Ana was not exactly known for her punctuality. Twirling her blonde hair around her fingers, Avery eyed up the menu. She had been coming to this same café for years now, and each time, she got the same breakfast. *Predictable Avery*, she thought to herself. But hey, she knew what she liked and stuck to it. There wasn't anything bad about that, right? Her thoughts were jogged by the arrival of a panting Ana with her long hair tied in a messy bun and her petite frame wrapped in a baggy jumper and black leggings. Ana rested her sunglasses atop her head.

Avery stood up to greet her sister. Ana made her apologies for being late and hugged Avery. Taking a step back, Avery stared at her sister. "Ana, you reek of alcohol." She looked at her younger sister up and down.

Flustered, Ana sat down and fanned herself with the menu. "Sue me," she replied, trying to act cool when part of her was freaking out for being so careless. This was bound to get back to her mother. Avery sat down looking at her sister disapprovingly.

"So have you been drinking all night, or did you wake up and start drinking?" she asked, almost afraid of the answer she would receive.

Ana glared at her and called the waitress. They sat in silence until their order was taken. A decaf coffee soon arrived for Ana, and she began to take a sip.

"Ana," Avery said, breaking the silence. A frosty tone rang in her voice. "How does a sixteen-year-old get drunk in this town?" she asked sincerely. They lived in a small town where everyone knew each other, Sure, she could have had a fake ID, but someone would know how old Anastasia was.

Ana refused to answer and continued to drink her coffee.

"What is going on with you?" Avery asked, frustrated at the indifference her sister showed.

"What do you care?" Ana retorted, angry that this nice breakfast with her sister was being ruined by an inquisition.

"I care!" Avery shouted somewhat defensively, her delicate features reddening. It was unlike her to show her emotions, especially when it came to anger. But something about Ana and her lack of care caused a fire inside Avery. Sophia had regularly called Avery while she was at university to talk about her concern for the wayward Ana. It was not fair to their mother for her reckless sister to cause such worry.

"Oh, you do?" Ana said in a sarcastic tone. "Since you left for UBC, there's not really been much caring from your side."

Avery sat back in her seat; she had been taken by surprise to hear Ana's view on her moving. They had never gotten the chance to talk that much. For years now, Ana had been slowly pulling away from everyone, including her. It made Avery sad to see their once-close bond become so distant. Maybe this was her opportunity to find out why.

"I'm sorry, Ana," she said quietly. "I guess I've had a lot going on." She tried to explain but Ana raised her hand to stop her.

"Oh, please. We all have a lot going on," she sneered and put her sunglasses back on her face. This was the mask she had to wear to act cool when she was afraid she would burst into tears.

"Ana, what is going on? Please . . . why are you so distant?" Avery reached across the table to hold her sister's hand, but Ana pulled away.

"Maybe this is who I've always been," Ana replied, trying to sound uninterested.

Avery shook her head. "Even you know that's not true. You're changing so much I don't know who you are anymore. Do you even know who you are?"

Their conversation was broken up by the arrival of their food. Ana spread butter on her toast and took a bite. In an almost synchronized way, Avery did the same. Both sisters caught sight of each other and giggled.

"See, no matter how hard we try, we'll always be in sync." Avery giggled, pinching Ana's nose like she did when they were kids. Ana laughed and did the same back to her sister. "Are you in trouble?" Avery asked, a serious look washing over her face.

Ana shook her head. "No. I'm not in trouble. I'm not going through a phase. I'm just being sixteen. Trying to have fun." Ana recited the same answer she gave their mother every time she would accuse Ana of falling off the rails.

"I worry, you know," Avery said, knowing it was falling on deaf ears.

Ana nodded and continued eating her food.

"Have you been going to therapy?" Avery asked.

Ana sighed. She was tired of people watching her like she was a ticking time bomb. Therefore, her secret life was secret. If people knew what she was up to, they would probably walk her straight into a detox facility. She had given up on therapy a few months ago. She got tired of being asked how she felt or if she still had her recurring nightmares. The answers were always the same. Yes, of course she did. They were called recurring nightmares for a reason. She knew she was numbing her pain through alcohol and drugs. She knew she was using her body to find the love she could not seem to feel. She knew she was self-destructing.

Unlike Avery, who needed to talk through everything, Ana preferred to self-medicate without the attention of medical professionals. After trying therapy for a year, she found it was not for her. Ana was very self-aware, not that it was doing her any good right now. Still, she understood the guilt Avery felt. It was no real secret that Ana felt resentment toward her older sister. She got up and left home the second she could, using university as an excuse to escape the nightmare town that held so many bad memories. Despite this, Ana understood. She would have done the same.

Maybe she was being overly harsh to her sister. It was not Avery's fault Ana was so messed up in the head. In fact, Ana knew deep down that if she even shared half the things going on inside her mind, Avery would do anything she could to help. But still, this was Ana's battle and hers alone. She hadn't always felt that way, especially when she first told the truth about what happened to her when she was twelve. But things were different now. She was different. No matter how hard anyone tried to understand or help, she was the one who would go to bed at night afraid of the haunting dreams she knew would come, the one who would close her eyes and feel the true coldness of the world. It was Ana and Ana alone who would vomit whenever the smell of oil and dirt filled her nostrils and only her who felt unclean whenever she got close to anyone at all. How could anyone help the huge lack of injustice Anastasia felt knowing her grandfather only got probation for molesting her, an innocent child who trusted him so completely? How could there be no justice served for stealing a child's innocence? Ana and Ana alone lived with this and it was up to her to handle it the way *she* wanted.

Sometimes, Ana thought this was not a world she wanted to live in. No amount of therapy would ever change this fact. Ana often thought to herself, *is that the going punishment these days for destroying a child's innocence? For tearing all the peace, love, and trust you're supposed to have in the people closest to you? Is probation the only punishment you get for stealing the innocence from someone's childhood?*

When Ana forgot all the horrible things that happened for so many years, she also forgot many of the good memories. Her childhood was robbed from her, and he got off punishment-free. Where was the justice in that? How can a person move on without justice? The thought that brought Anastasia to her knees was that she always had a big bright light inside of her filled with wonder, love, and happiness, and *he* blew it out. Now Ana felt like a shell of her former self. Though she tried hard to keep up her nonchalance, a tear fell down her face. Unfortunately, Avery had been watching her intently.

"I want to be here for you. You just have to let me in," Avery said, once again reaching out for her sister. This time, Ana let her clasp her hand.

"I think I'm too far gone," Ana admitted, her lip quivering, more tears threatening to fall.

"No, you're not," Avery replied, tears streaming down her face. "You are not alone in this; Mom and I are always here for you!" Avery shook Ana's hand to reinforce her support for her sister. Ana nodded and squeezed her sister's hand. She had been doing this whole "I'm fine. I don't need help" act for so long that sometimes it felt nice to know someone was on her side. She knew the demons were still lingering, but right there, with her sister, she knew there were going to be good days to make up for the dark ones. Ana's family was everything to her, and she knew they would always be there for her, just as they have been since that day she spoke her truth.

* * *

What was it about Carter that Ana loved so much? Was it the way he looked like a young James Dean, or was it how despite his tough, cool guy exterior, she knew how poetic his heart was? They had known each other for years now, bonded through their past experiences of abuse, and united by the feeling of abandonment. Carter was eighteen years old when she had met him in a club on one of her nights out. He had wooed her with champagne and weed, progressing to cocaine and ecstasy. He lived a fast life full of parties, drugs, alcohol, and sex. He was popular. In fact, Ana was just a shy girl wanting to rebel when she met him. He taught her how to use her body to get whatever she wanted, taught her to feel confident and beautiful. Ana had looked up to him. She wanted to be with him, but he kept her at arm's length. Deep down, she knew he was not good for her, but she loved him despite that. She loved the affection he gave her. She was young, naive, and let Carter get whatever he wanted, including her. She knew she was vulnerable. Perhaps that was the reason why he refused to be serious with her.

If age was the problem, then he should have said something back when they first met when he spotted her fake ID from a mile away. He had his own fake ID from the same place she had gotten hers. Her lack of knowledge when it came to choosing a drink also showed her inexperience with the nightlife in Vancouver. He had taught her everything he knew, including how to pleasure a man. Ana had been relatively innocent when they met, and she certainly hadn't been into BDSM. But she had been eager to please him, and she was willing. No matter what he did to her, she would come back wanting more. He thought she was great company because she was always so willing to boost his ego every time he felt down. Deep down, they both knew it was a toxic relationship.

But they were able to share secrets with each other they had not dared to share with anyone else. Ana loved him and would do anything for him.

He was the one person outside of her family she had shared her secrets with. He taught her how drugs could numb the pain, in turn showing her the scars he had gotten from the beatings he took from his alcoholic father and the cigarette marks his drug addict mother had left on his body. Both were undeniably broken, never really healing and always masking the pain behind a life filled with sex, drugs, and alcohol. He always had a front seat at all the best parties and clubs in the amazing downtown vibe of Vancouver.

Carter took great care of Ana, showing her a tenderness she did not realize she was desperate for. But he had a violent streak; a rage deep inside him burned from the years of abuse he had endured. He held anger toward the establishment. Professionals turned a blind eye as ten-year-old Carter turned up to school bruised and bloodied. All the kids called him names and said he was dirty because his clothes had not been washed in weeks. All the women who had used and abused him, all the managers who called him stupid, all the friends who had abandoned him. Through the years, Ana was the only one who stayed. He often thought that it was because she might not have anywhere else to go. But that did not matter because he did not have anywhere else to turn either.

He had spent years building himself up. He fancied himself as a young entrepreneur. Sure, it was more underground stuff that he was working on. But at eighteen years old, he was making great money selling drugs to old businessmen who had bigger problems than him. He could afford to fund his expensive lifestyle without having to work in a stuffy office or stacking shelves. Did this make him happy? Absolutely not. He was empty. No matter how hard he tried to fill himself up with alcohol, drugs, or women, nothing ever satisfied him. But that did not stop him from trying.

They had just finished making love when Ana turned to him. Her bright blue eyes glistened as she took a drag from his joint. Swigging her beer, she sighed.

"Why can't every day be like this?" she asked him, thoughtfully staring up at the ceiling as she watched the car lights reflect around the room through the window.

Carter sat up, naked on the edge of the bed, and took a gulp from his bottle. He hated when Ana got herself into one of her daydreams. More of a realist, he did not enjoy participating in her fantasies.

"Because we've got shit to do," he responded gruffly. Ana laughed, not picking up on his tone. She continued watching the lights dance, her head feeling dizzy, but she was enjoying it.

"Carter . . ." she mumbled, nudging him with her toes. "I love you," she said, feeling herself blush as soon as she said it.

Carter lit up a cigarette and did not respond.

"Hey!" Ana shouted, counting the number of times the room went into complete darkness.

"Hey, what?" Carter replied, taking a deep drag.

"I said I love you," Ana shouted again, sounding like a petulant kid.

"So what?" he said, taking another drink from his beer.

Ana gathered the white sheets around her naked body and stood up angrily, her high starting to take a negative turn. She threw a pillow at his head, causing the neck of his bottle to go a little too far into his mouth. Carter bit his lip.

"For fuck's sake, what the hell is wrong with you?" he asked her, turning around to face the upset Ana.

"I told you I love you and you respond with 'so what?' Who do you think you are?" Ana said loudly, hearing her voice echo in her ears.

"What do you want me to say? 'I love you too. Let's go get married'?" he replied in a sarcastic tone, causing Ana to get even angrier.

"Well, it would not hurt for you to take me seriously sometimes!"

Carter sighed, taking a long puff and exhaling sharply. "Take you seriously? You're just a fucking kid, Ana." He laughed, throwing the pillow back at her. Ana leaped across the bed and faced Carter.

"I'm not a kid. I haven't been a *kid* in a very long time," she insisted, beginning to feel tears sting her eyes. *How could he be so cold when she just professed her true feelings for him?*

"Stop using me for emotional comfort. I told you I'm not interested," Carter said coldly, throwing her a disgusted look.

Ana's eyes filled with tears, and she screamed out in frustration. "How come I'm good enough for you to fuck but not good enough for you to love?" Ana asked, clenching her fist into tight balls.

"You're working yourself up. You're doing this to yourself. Calm down." Carter laughed at her, surprised at how much of a child she was being. "Stop telling me what to do!" Ana cried, pushing him away from her. She could tell he was trying to rattle her, get her to say something she would regret.

"You're disgusting." She spat out the words like they were venom in her mouth. His demeanor changed, and his face got serious.

"And you're so broken no one will ever want you. Do you think I'd want to have an underage slut as a girlfriend?" he retorted, sneering at her.

Ana saw red as she tried to compose herself, standing up so she towered above his sitting body. Ana looked at him straight in the eyes. "You don't mean that." Tears now streamed down her cheeks; her sobs were silent aside from the occasional hiccup.

Carter sneered again. He was winning, and that was all that mattered. "Of course, I mean it. I call it how I see it. You think you're so cool and rebellious going out every night partying hard? No, you're so desperate for the love no one will give you that you're willing to put out to anyone who says hello." He laughed again, watching as her face contorted to avoid showing more emotions than her tears gave away.

"I know you'll be sorry tomorrow, Carter," she said again, the gentleness of her voice breaking ever so slightly.

"The only thing I'm sorry for is taking pity on such a pathetic loser like you. You're wasted goods, Ana. I could never love someone as desperate as you." Carter howled with laughter as he threw himself back down onto his bed with his arms casually behind his head. He looked so smug that Ana walked so quickly over to him to argue but was stopped short. He moved so fast, she didn't expect the blow that came next when he hit her clear across the face, causing her to land on the floor. She lay bleeding and hurt while he stood there laughing at her. She never felt so used. Ana cried out in disbelief as she gently touched her fingers to the cut on her cheekbone. He hit her hard enough to draw blood. She quickly dressed as Carter laughed louder at her crying in despair.

"Oh, come on, Ana. You're acting as if any of this is news to you!" Grabbing her stuff, Ana walked out the door, leaving behind the sound of Carter hysterically laughing to himself. With tears in her eyes, a bloody lip, and her chest thumping so hard she could hear it, Ana ran home to find some peace in the pain that was consuming her.

* * *

Ana lit the candles and ran the bath. She dipped her fingers into the running water under the tub's faucet. The temperature was perfect, a little cooler than scalding but hot enough to cause her mild discomfort. She had always loved soaking her body in hot water, so hot it would cause her skin to go red. It was the one way she knew she was clean after every time grandpa abused her and she hoped that now it would soothe the pain that Carter had inflicted earlier in the day. Ana put her hair up in a bun to stop it from getting wet and eased her body gently into the water. Tears were still streaming down her face, but her sobs were silent so as not to disturb the silence she wanted to surround her. Not that it would have mattered if she screamed and raged; her mother had gone to stay with her aunt, so Ana had the house to herself.

Ana's heart hurt; deep pain had followed her for years. There were times when she felt so alone that she only had her pain and trauma to keep her company. She could never express just how badly she felt inside like she was constantly drinking poison. Inside her was darkness. Sometimes she felt empty, while other times she was so full of anger and sorrow that she found herself feeling lightheaded.

Ana let herself fall deeper into the tub. She'd gone through times in her life where she would come up with her own remedies for the evil she felt inside of her. For years, she had hidden the true depth of her despair. People often asked why she had drifted away from everything she had known. Perhaps it was the years of exile she put herself under. Sure, she chose to exile herself, but could anyone blame her? Her abuser, her own grandfather, went unpunished for the years of torment he put her through. His court-appointed AA meetings went unchecked, so he continued to live his life, drinking and laughing without ever attending a single meeting. He got to enjoy the family gatherings she had once loved going to. It was like she, the victim, was the only one punished. Everyone got to live their life their own way, but Ana, from a young age, had learned to be silent. She felt like life had failed her, and no matter how hard she tried, it kept failing her.

Carter was right. She was looking for love in all the wrong places. Ana knew two things: how to use her body to get what she wanted and being betrayed by those she loved; that hurt the worst. She was only good for one thing, and so of course, that one thing would be the first thing she would offer. Maybe he was right about everything. Maybe there really would be no one who would ever want her because she was broken goods. Maybe life really was just harsh, and she would never be able to escape the trauma of her past. Maybe the light that people used to tell her radiated from within her really was gone? Maybe this was as good as it was going to get. Ana cried deeper, finally letting her sobs echo around the bathroom. She held her breath and dunked herself under the water. Staring up at the ceiling above her, she let the water wash over her eyes. Refusing to blink, she kept herself under, using her hands to keep herself below the water. She felt the need to take a breath, but she refused to let herself back up for air.

Maybe today was the day that the pain would finally go away. Maybe the world would be a better place without her. Maybe she would never heal. Maybe her grandfather would forever haunt her nightmares. Ana felt faint but still. She dug her nails onto the edge of the tub, refusing to let herself take another breath.

The pain covered each and every part of her body: the trauma, each memory etched into her skin with scars to remind her of the very worst parts; the nightmares, always haunting her only safe space; her dreams, never letting her rest and never letting her forget. Life had been hard for so long that she forgot what it felt like to be happy and carefree. She never truly had a childhood, and her adolescence felt like it would only bring more horror. She thought about her family. *Would her mother have to forever feel obligated to look after such a messed-up daughter? Would Avery be followed by the dark cloud Ana brought with her? Would her father continue to feel the guilt of not being able to protect her?* She thought about her future children. *Could they be punished or affected in some way by the parts of Ana that refused to heal?* Then she thought about herself and how hard she'd fought from a young age to lead a normal life. How much she wanted to experience life without pain holding her back. Ana wanted to live, to show the world that despite the challenges thrown at her, and the injustice, she could overcome and succeed. Rising from the water, Ana took gulping breaths. She did want to live. She just didn't know how.

* * *

Bussing tables, taking orders, and picking up checks. It was the same shift, just a different day for Ana. She was exhausted, weary, and feeling hopeless. Time was moving so slow, and yet Ana was losing track of the days. Classes were quick; the time at home was even quicker. Lately, Ana had been keeping to herself, keeping her head down. It had been a week since she last spoke to Carter, seven days since she had contemplated taking her own life for the first time. She was keeping focused on earning her money and someday saving enough to just disappear. To where? She had no idea. Perhaps somewhere far away, somewhere beautiful, somewhere where nobody knew her.

Just like she did every day, Grace came through the diner doors smiling at Ana as she took her seat in her regular spot. Ana followed to take her order.

"Are we still pretending that you're not here for your usual, Grace?" Ana laughed, taking a seat opposite her friend.

Grace chuckled and nodded. "One day, I might surprise you and ask for something different!" she joked.

Ana put her hand up to her forehead and pretended to faint. "Oh, don't. You're the one constant I look forward to every day!" Ana laughed, nodding to the chef behind the counter to signal they were good to go on Grace's regular order.

"So, dear, how are you today?" Grace asked, a concern washing over her face. Since they officially made friends, Grace had been a friendly and non-judgmental shoulder to lean on. Ana had been surprised at how easy it was to speak to her older friend, despite generations between them. If only Grace was her age. They would for sure make a dangerous and powerful team. While there were a lot of things that Ana had kept to herself, she had confided in Grace about most of her relationships, including her relationship with Carter. In fact, Grace was the only person she'd spoken to about the argument she had with him. Grace sat, listened, and comforted Ana but only gave one piece of advice.

"You don't belong in a place that gives you so much pain, my dear." She patted Ana's shaking hand. "Love isn't meant to be that hard, and if it is, then it isn't love."

Grace had been a great source of comfort for Ana over the past few weeks. Ana was surprised by the relationship that developed between them because she did not tend to be friends or take the time to know the elderly. Her friendship with Grace also helped her realize that she avoided relationships with older people because of her childhood experience, but Grace was different. Grace shared with Ana the inspiring stories of her career and spoke about the challenges she had to go through to climb the career ladder; she enjoyed breaking the glass ceiling as often as she could. Ana could only dream of being such a high-powered career woman like Grace. If she allowed herself to daydream about a different life, Ana dreamed of being just like Grace when she was her age, having enough money to be able to be anywhere in the world but choosing to be in this small little town talking to a young stranger who had clearly lost their way. Ana dreamed she would someday be able to make a difference in someone's life one day. But that was only a secret dream she knew would never happen. She would live and die in this backward town full of pain that both kept her here and made her want to run away.

Ana stayed and chatted with Grace as they caught up on the gossip from Grace's gardening club, the kinds of books she had picked up from the bookstore, and what kinds of classes Ana was planning on taking next year. Sensing something was preoccupying her young friend's mind, Grace reached out and held Ana's hand. Ana flinched for a moment, an instinct she had picked up from when she was a kid. Ana smiled apologetically and held on to Grace.

"What's on your mind?" Grace asked kindly.

Tears once again filled Ana's eyes as she quietly whispered about the darkness she had been feeling. A part of her wanted to be honest about her past, wanted to let this ugly secret out to someone she trusted, but Ana knew better than to do that. She knew that the moment she shared her past she would be weak once more. But was she ever really strong? If she was strong, she would not be afraid to go to certain parts of town without fear she would run into her grandfather.

Though she had done her best to avoid him, she was still haunted by the occasions from her childhood when she would be carefree, gallivanting around town with friends and seeing him in the distance. If she was strong, she should be able to tell her mother of the pain she was still carrying and share why she felt so lost and distant. If she was strong, she should be able to hold herself to a higher value and not let people like Carter tell her she was worthless. She should believe it when people like Grace told her she could do anything in this world. But she did not feel strong, especially now. She was Anastasia, the girl abused by her grandfather, and that was something she could never change. For as long as she was in this town, she would be forever reminded of the kid who did not know any better and was taken advantage of. She would be reminded of a justice system that protected a predator over an innocent child, of all the family parties, special occasions where she lay in her bed crying as her mother comforted her. Ana was always reminded of this one party where she finally dared to stand up for herself. She always hated walking in the front door knowing what was coming next: *him*. He would come in search of whoever arrived to give them a big sloppy kiss and hug, which she had endured every visit. It had her secretly running to the bathroom to clean her face.

But the last time was different. Instead of trying to avoid him, she walked right up to his face and said "No" loudly, and the whole family had taken notice. The look of shock had been worth it. For the first time, she felt empowered and allowed herself to continue. "No, I don't want you to kiss me. You've done enough of that. I don't want your hands touching me. You've done enough of that too. Just *no*. Don't ever touch or kiss me again."

She had heard that there are moments in our lives that shape who we are. That moment, when she finally stood up to him, was one of those moments for her. She felt so proud of herself, realizing that she no longer had to try and hide from the affection that he had no right to give to her anymore. He took enough from her; his reign over her, as far as she was concerned, was over! The courts may not have given her the justice she deserved, but at that moment, she was the judge, the jurors, and the executioner. She remembered the look on his face as she walked right past him to where her family gathered, looking a little shocked. As soon as Ana came in with a huge smile on her face, it was like they were all on pause, Ana pressed play, and the whole group started moving again. Ana let out a huge breath she did not realize she was holding, but when she looked up, expecting to see confusion, perhaps even sadness in her family's eyes, she only saw love and understanding. Ana really did have an amazing family; sure, they still got together with their aging parents and that was something she never could understand. But it did not matter. They supported her and loved her. Now she was setting the tone; she was happy and could enjoy the day, on her terms and in a way that made her feel comfortable. However, he would remain the creator of her pain. He created this life she now felt stuck in.

"Sometimes I wish I could just disappear or run away," she finally said, putting her hands under the table and pinching herself.

"And what good would that do?" Grace asked. If anyone else asked this question, Ana would think they were being argumentative, but she knew Grace asked to get Ana to question herself.

"Then maybe I could start fresh . . . have a chance to be somebody else."

"But there's nothing wrong with who you are now," Grace replied simply, shaking her head. She put a delicate finger on Ana's chin and lifted it up so they were eye to eye. "Never apologize for who you are and what you've experienced. Use it as your motivation to do better and be better than anyone else expected of you. Don't do it for them, but do it for you."

Ana nodded and smiled at Grace. She had a way with words, never judging Ana for her way of thinking or assuming that she was only acting this way because she was a teenager. Grace took her seriously, understood her pain without needing to know the whole story.

"I once ran away, you know," Grace said, looking out of the window. Ana had learned that was her favorite pastime. "Ran away to Seattle to see the Emerald City." Grace's eyes glistened as she shared a few stories of her time in Seattle, the people she met, the opportunities she discovered, and most importantly, how they helped her realize what she was looking for in life. "I found myself there. If ever you get a chance, you should visit too. You never know what you might find." Grace looked back at Ana and tucked her hair away from her face. Grace saw herself in Ana. Ana had a thirst for knowledge and adventure, much like Grace did when she was younger. Both had difficult starts in their lives, and many years of life had taught Grace that only the strong survived in this world. From what she could see and what she knew of Anastasia Rose, she was one strong girl. Ana just didn't know it yet. But she would. Grace was confident about that.

* * *

Ana watched Haven pull her miniskirt down to cover more of her legs. She stood next to Ana in the chilly, night air as her friend lit up one of her joints. It'd been some time since they indulged in their reckless nights out and it was much needed now. Ana danced around the smoking area, sashaying her way around those standing around getting fresh air. Tonight, she felt carefree and happy. She was with her best friend, she was drunk, and she was having the time of her life. Haven danced beside her, her true partner in crime. So far tonight, they had managed to swing themselves a free night out. Drinks were endless, and the good times kept rolling in. Ana was fighting a spiral into her depression that she was placating with alcohol. *Typical Ana, running away from her problems instead of facing them*, she thought to herself as she downed yet another shot from a random stranger who clearly had bad intentions. After taking her drink, she moved on, pulling Haven back onto the dance floor. Dancing her troubles away was her favorite form of therapy. It made her look good, feel better, and helped her hide behind a mask of confidence.

    From behind her, Carter appeared and pulled her to him. Caught by surprise, Ana pushed him away. She had nothing to say to him. Trying to walk away, Carter forcefully pulled her to him again. Haven rolled her eyes and tried to pull Ana away, but Carter stood between them. Putting a middle finger up at Haven, Carter turned his back to her and faced Ana again. The music was loud; she could not hear what he was saying. Ana could tell from looking at his eyes that he was high on coke again. She watched his lips mouth a load of garbled words. She didn't want to listen to what he had to say. He didn't deserve her time anymore. Ana tried to move away from him again, but he kept grabbing her. He put his hands on her face and mouthed, "I'm sorry." Ana shook her head and finally pulled free from him and went to look for Haven.

    Haven was at the bar when Ana joined her. "Keep me away from that jerk," Ana asked her friend as they ordered their drinks. Haven nodded in agreement. Two guys approached them, and Ana felt her good time mask slip back on. After a few minutes of flirting, Haven was making out with her guy as Ana and the new guy, Ryan, continued chatting awkwardly beside them. She felt no real spark with this guy, but she put up with him for the sake of Haven's hookup. Ryan was a nice enough guy, but there was something about the way he looked at Ana that made her feel uncomfortable. It was rare for Ana, while in her confident persona, to be made to feel like she wanted to fade into the background. He observed her like he was trying to figure her out. She looked over at Haven and her hookup. It didn't look like they were going to come up for air anytime soon, so Ana grabbed the back of Ryan's head and pulled him to her. They kissed, but with no romantic feelings on her part, Ana was just bored. *Why was he kissing weird?*

"Oh, god," Ana accidentally said out loud. Thankfully her voice came out sounding more excited and sexual than annoyed, due to all the practice she's had in making out in clubs. She realized that he was most likely a virgin. Ana did not like that. There was no way she would be taking it any further than kissing. Yeah, she was a little messed up but not that messed up. She was not prepared to be a mistake for him. Ryan was nervous; she could tell from the way he trembled underneath her touch. In another life, he would probably have made a decent guy to bring home to her mom. She could have probably fallen in love with him. Maybe he would encourage her to go to college, travel the world together, settle down somewhere abroad, and have a bunch of kids together. Ana allowed herself to get caught up in her daydream.

The next thing she knew, Ryan was being pulled away from her. Carter's face popped up in a flash and drinks started being thrown around. Ryan and Carter were caught up in a brawl. Haven's hookup pulled away from her to help his friend, and before they knew it, a full fight, involving many innocent bystanders, broke out. Glass was shattered, and at one point, Ana found herself trying to pull Carter off Ryan's friend. Somewhere in the scuffle, Ana's face got cut by a stray piece of broken champagne bottle. She felt no pain as the drugs had kicked in, making her feel numb. The music stopped at the club and the lights were turned on, but this did not stop the fight. The small brawl quickly escalated until police sirens rang out. Ana lost sight of Haven and found her hair being pulled by a random girl who seemed hell-bent on getting involved. Bloodied and bruised, Ana was then grabbed from behind. Defending herself, she turned and punched the stranger in the nose, only to realize, to her horror, that it was a police officer.

Handcuffed, Ana was ushered out along with many other patrons of the club, seeing in the crowd a horrified Haven watching her friend be taken away by police.

Chapter 7

Sophia sat silently watching her bloodied daughter stare at her fingers. They had been sitting at the kitchen table for thirty minutes in complete silence. Sophia was biding her time, trying to calm herself down. Ana knew she had it coming.

"You're sixteen, Ana! Sixteen, and tonight, I had to bail you out of jail," she said, finally unleashing her anger. "What the hell is going on? How can I help you if you won't talk to me?" Sophia felt frustrated. Her daughter had been pulling away for years, and her psychology degree could only help so much with navigating through the difficult teen years. Ana had the usual signs that children who have been abused exhibited; those were easy to identify. It was the ones that she had not been warned about that left her stumped. Ana had never been so reckless. In fact, she had isolated herself after the traumatic events of her childhood. Sophia feared she would become a mute or a complete recluse, so she thanked the heavens when Ana had started participating in regular teenage activities. She seemed popular in school, she was intelligent, often getting top marks in class, and yet, there was a side to her daughter she knew nothing about. It was like, after dark, someone completely different took over Anastasia.

"I'm sorry, mom," Ana whimpered, knowing that she was causing her mother an immense amount of stress that she did not deserve.

"Am I such a terrible mother, Ana?" Sophia questioned.

Ana shook her head.

"Then why are you doing this to me?" Exhausted, Sophia put her head in her hands.

"I don't know," Ana whispered, afraid to say something wrong.

"That's not a good enough answer, Anastasia Rose. We need to communicate. I need to know how I am supposed to help you because lord knows I'm trying my best to understand."

"I don't know what's wrong with me, Mom," Ana said, finally trying to reach out to her mother. Sophia burst into tears. It had been a long four years living with a dark cloud above their heads. There were times when Sophia thought they were finally making headway, that Ana was finally ready to start healing from her past trauma, then something like this would happen and Sophia would be left confused, unsure of whether they were making real progress anymore. It was taking a toll. Yet, she felt like she never had a right to complain. She was not the victim. She did not suffer the same pain, but she had a right to feel hurt and frustrated too, right?

"You're drinking, you're reckless, you're running wild and living a life I know nothing about . . ." Sophia counted every wrongdoing on her fingers. "When you're home, you're basically a ghost, you're not interested in being part of this family . . ."

"No, it's not that, Mom." Ana tried to argue back. "I want to be a part of this family. I just don't feel like I belong." There, she finally said something she had been keeping inside of her for so long.

"Do I not make you feel wanted?" Sophia looked hurt; tears started to well up.

"It's not that, Mom. It's nothing you've done. It's me. I'm the problem." Ana began crying too. She hated it when she saw her mother in so much pain. She hated that she caused the hurt that filled her eyes. She had disappointed her mother yet again.

Sophia stood up and made her way to her daughter. She cradled Ana's head in her arms and rocked her lightly.

"Ana, you are not a problem. You are not the problem. You're hurting, and I don't know how, but I promise it will all be okay one day."

Mother and daughter cried as they held each other in the kitchen where so many big moments in their lives happened. Happy, sad, painful, and momentous moments. This house was filled with so much love, and yet, it also held so many painful secrets for Ana. Every nook, every cranny, every inch of her childhood home held scarring stories that haunted Ana every time she walked through those front doors. For the longest time, it was comforting to have her mother by her side to talk to, to cry with, to laugh alongside, but at that moment, as they held each other, Ana realized it no longer felt like home.

* * *

Ana had taken an early shift at the diner which meant she and Grace would only have a short time together before she would have to head to her study session with her project teammates in biology. Watching the clock, Ana realized she had been waiting for Grace to come in much more than she was looking forward to clocking off for the day. She had gotten so used to seeing her friend at the diner that if she didn't have work, it felt strange not seeing Grace.

Grace's friendly face popped through the door as she beamed straight at Ana, nodding to the chef to get her order ready, Ana put her apron behind the counter and made her way over to what had become their table. Ana took her usual spot as Grace faced her favorite window. Ana had been wanting to share some realizations she'd had about her life as well as to tell her about the dream board she had been making to finally have a place for her daydreams to go.

Ana chatted animatedly as Grace listened intently while drinking her water. The two friends exchanged stories from their last few days. When Grace's food finally came, Ana patiently waited for Grace to take a few bites before continuing with her daydream.

"My dear, call it your plans for the future!" Grace smiled, eager to help Ana realize that she was capable of much more than just daydreaming.

"Oh no, Grace. They're way too big for me." Ana blushed. She had never admitted that a small part of her dreamed big and wished for it to come true.

"What? Too big for an ambitious girl like you?" Grace questioned, raising her eyebrow and looking at Ana with interest.

Ana lowered her head. "Let's face it. I'll be stuck here forever. It's just fun to pretend that someday I'll get to be an important businesswoman like you."

Grace shook her head. "You've got brains, you've got sass, and you are passionate. Those are qualities of a future leader, Anastasia. Why do you talk down about yourself like this?"

Ana looked up surprised, no one had ever asked her that question before. She did not have a sarcastic response ready. She shrugged. "People like me, we're not expected to achieve much." She replied, lowering her head. Grace gently put her hand under Ana's chin and raised her head, looking straight into her eyes.

Grace whispered what she said next so only they could hear. "People like you are born to change this world, Ana. If you stop doubting yourself, then maybe you would start to see that. Stop saying you're stuck because you're not. You're just afraid to fail, but darling, what if you surprise yourself and succeed, then what?"

Taking a deep breath of air, an idea suddenly came to Ana like it had been there all along. She was never going anywhere while she felt trapped by her past. She had bad relationships and made many mistakes, and it was only because she believed that was all life had to offer her. She did not know it until that moment, but she had been biding her time until she either got so miserable that she killed herself or for some kind of miracle to happen that would jump-start her life. She had been hiding behind her pain because it was all she had known. She only knew what it meant to survive and never really tried to thrive.

She'd had enough. She did not want to be a victim anymore. She was done being poor little "Ana-Cakes." She wanted to stop seeing the sad faces of the people who knew her past. She wanted to stop feeling like the town was whispering about her. For once, she wanted to only meet strangers who had no clue who she was and the trauma that happened to her.

Ana picked up her phone and texted Haven. In typical Haven fashion, her response came within seconds: *I'm in!*

* * *

Haven parked her car in Ana's driveway and ran through the front door. They were not in a rush as Sophia would not be back until the evening, but adrenaline rushed through their veins at the thought of what they were about to do. Haven ran up to Ana's room, the same room she had since she was a kid. Even though it still looked like the room of a teenager, Ana's room still had remnants from her childhood. Old photographs, paintings, and school awards plastered her room. Ana looked around, her memories from her entire life were in this room. Yes, many were awful, but there were some amazing ones too. Taking a deep breath, she kept telling herself this was the only way she would finally be able to live her life free of the pain, free of the past, free of the memories, and free of Carter.

"Are you sure you want to do this?" Ana asked Haven for what felt like the hundredth time. Haven had barely been there five minutes, but Ana's anxiety was starting to rub off on her.

"Yes, yes, and when you ask me again in a minute, it will still be yes." Haven laughed as she helped Ana pack up her clothes. Going around her room touching memorabilia and trinkets, Ana wondered whether any of her stuff was worth taking with her. In the end, she decided that all she really needed was her clothes and her favorite picture that had the smiling faces of her mom, Avery, and a young Ana. Everything else could stay right where it was.

Ana's heart beat loudly. She was finally doing it. She was finally running away, leaving the past behind and starting a new life. Or so she hoped.

Ana and Haven packed up Haven's car with only a suitcase for each of them. The girls held hands and made their way onto the open road.

"Ana . . . where exactly are we going?" Haven asked, suddenly realizing that she had agreed to leave her life behind and move without really knowing their destination. Even though she trusted Ana, Haven still needed to know where they were going since she was the one driving.

Ana laughed and took Haven's hand once again and intertwined her fingers with her best friends. "To Seattle!" Ana shouted, getting Haven hyped up. The girls screamed and sped their little Mini Cooper down the road while Ana watched Vancouver get smaller in the rear view mirror. She rolled down her window and put her head out to let the wind whip her long blonde hair around. Ana felt alive for the first time in a long time! Haven was laughing as she kept glancing at her friend. Ana felt so free as she thought, *Let the adventure begin.*

* * *

They had barely driven an hour when Haven realized she needed to stop for gas. Pulling up to the next service station, Ana jumped out of the car to use the toilet while Haven filled the gas tank.

As Ana made her way into the store, she caught sight of a familiar face. "Ana?" the voice called out before walking toward her.

"Dad, is that you?" Ana replied, shocked. Her face told Robert she was doing something she should not be.

"Are you off on a trip?" he asked, still surprised to see his daughter so far from home.

"Yes, sort of . . ." Ana said, squirming. She was never a very good liar, especially when it came to her father.

"Where are you going?" Feeling his fatherly instincts kick in, he was sure that Ana was up to something she should not be doing.

Ana shrugged her shoulders and tried to change the subject, but Robert was not having it. He could not shake the thought that she was in trouble. Knowing her father was not going to budge from his questioning, Ana pulled him to the chairs in the corner of the store. Together they sat down as Ana explained what she was doing. She could not keep her move from her father. Part of her was hoping he could be the one who could break the news to her mother. Robert sighed, looking at Ana's eyes to see if there were any signs she was not herself, but he only saw the determination etched in her face.

"But Ana . . . you're only sixteen . . ." He tried to reason with her, but Ana shook her head.

"Let's face it, Dad. I haven't been a little girl in a long time," she stated, knowing he would understand what she was trying to say.

"And you think this will make you happy?" he asked, wanting some reassurance that she wasn't just being irresponsible. Ana told her dad about the realizations she had been having and the despair she found herself in that led up to her decision to make this big move to Seattle. She reassured him she was with her best friend and that they had a plan. She promised she would stay in touch. Robert could see the despair in her eyes. He could see her need to do this, but one thing he knew for certain, he was not letting her leave without calling her mother. Robert knew Sophia would never let him live it down, so he handed his phone to Ana and demanded that she call her mother right away. "Call your mother and tell her Ana, or you aren't going anywhere. Your mother loves you, and she will be devastated." Ana knew what he said was true but was so afraid that she would not be able to go through with her new adventure if she heard her mom's voice.

"Robert, is everything all right? Do you know where Ana is? I can't . . ." Sophia sounded frantic. Ana knew at that moment that she needed to tell her the truth.

"Mom, it's me." She was met by silence. "I am here with Dad. I'm leaving town. Haven and I are moving to Seattle," Ana rambled on scared of any silence for fear she wouldn't go through with it, knowing it was only her mother who could talk her out of this. Her mother was always on her side, supporting her through all the ups and downs. She was the one person she never wanted to hurt or let down but Ana also knew she needed to do this, for *herself*.

"What did you just say?" her mom asked, an octave higher than she meant as if she had misheard what her daughter had said. "Because I think I just heard you say you are moving, and you didn't even tell me or say goodbye. And oh yeah, you're sixteen!" her mom said hysterically.

"Mom, I am sorry. I know this is hard for you to hear, but I need to do this. I need to get away. I need a fresh start. Just for a while. I promise I'll call you every single day." Ana did not want to stop talking.

"Anastasia, please honey . . . I love you. Please don't . . . I'll be right there and we can talk . . ." Sophia's voice was strained. Ana knew she was crying.

"Mom, please stop. I love you so much. You are the best mother anyone could ever ask for. I know it's been hard these last few years, but Mom, things are bad with Carter. Things are *really* bad with me." She could hear her mom quietly crying.

"I know, baby girl. I know," was all Sophia could say. "Go find your light Anastasia and always remember how much I love you."

Ana started to cry. Her mom understood. They had always been close, but Ana was still determined to go especially after the scare she gave herself in the bathtub. She needed to get away, no matter how much it hurt her to leave her mom and family.

"I love you, Mom." Then she hung up. Her mind was swirling but before she could think of another thought, Robert embraced Ana tightly, catching her off guard as he moved to her so quickly. Ana was right. She had grown up a long time ago and was stronger than anyone he had ever known. The one thing she had been missing was her sense of identity. He looked at Ana again, searching for any sign that she was doing this as a cry for help. The strong-headed, determined girl he recognized from her childhood stood looking back at him.

"I need to do this, Dad. I need to find myself. I can't do that back home. I'll never escape my past, and I'll never have a future if I keep looking back," Ana told her father with certainty. Ana was a lot like Robert when it came to being stubborn, so he already knew by what she said to Sophia that nothing he could say could make her stay.

Robert walked Ana back to Haven's car where they hugged and said their goodbyes.

"Dad, stop. This isn't 'goodbye'; it's 'see you later'," Ana assured him, feeling her tears start to well up. Before she had second thoughts, she kissed her dad tenderly on his cheek and got into the car.

Robert put his head through the open window and kissed his daughter on her forehead and said quietly, so only she could hear, "Anastasia, my sweet, sweet daughter, you are such a strong woman, stronger than you know. So go now and start the life you were always meant to live and remember: never give up on yourself."

Ana put her sunglasses on so that Haven did not see the tears filling her eyes. She watched as her father disappeared from her mirror. She knew this was not goodbye, but she was not prepared for how hard it would be to see her hometown in the rearview mirror; it made her both excited and sad.

Ana was happy that she now essentially had her parents' blessing. She needed to get away from Carter; she needed to get away from it all and have a fresh start. She loved her parents, family, and friends, but it was the relationship with herself she needed to work on. As her father vanished from the rearview mirror, she noticed Haven had gotten very quiet, observing Ana to see if she had changed her mind. But Ana was determined.

"Ana, do you still wanna . . ." Ana put her hand up to silence her. She looked at her best friend, smiled, rolled down the windows, cranked up the music, and with her head once again out the window, started singing with the music. She was excited to be embarking on this new adventure. Talking to her parents had relieved pressure she didn't realize was there.

"Haven, turn up this song! I love it!"

"And girls just wanna have fun . . . oh girls, just wanna have . . . Sing with me, Haven!" Ana hollered, and the two girls rode into the sunset.

PART II:
Rising from the Ashes

CHAPTER 8

Ten years later

"Happy tenth anniversary!" Haven looked ravishing tonight with her six-inch black stilettos and ran to hug Ana Laughing, they both sat down at their table. Haven was the last one to arrive at their joint celebration. Their friends were already seated, sipping on their cocktails.

"Happy Anniversary to you too!" Ana said. Haven giggled, brushing her glowing blonde hair behind her ears to reveal her equally shining diamond earrings.

"Ohhh! Are they new?" Haven leaned across their friend Anthony and took his drink.

Ana twirled her hair around her finger and nodded. "A gift from my boss for our special day." Ana winked. Haven nodded, knowing exactly what that meant. Anthony stood up, ready to make a toast.

"It's been ten years since Seattle was hit by a big hurricane." The table went silent. They were a little confused but continued to listen to his loud but gentle voice. Anthony was handsome in his tailored navy suit. If his voice hadn't commanded everyone's attention, his physique would have. "It's been ten years since two young, wild women came to conquer our beautiful city." The table burst into laughter. "Ten years since two small-town girls made this city their home. I know I'm not the only one who is happy about that! Ana and Haven, we're all so glad you came into our lives and brought so much fun chaos with you!"

Everyone at the table raised their glasses and cheered as Haven downed her drink and Ana sipped, smiling into her glass. She didn't know how Haven was feeling. But she knew her friend well, and the fact that she was already tipsy meant she had felt nervous about the memories of leaving Maple Ridge flooding back. Ana had been far too busy with work to think about how different life had been ten years ago.

Back then, they were two lost teenagers who had no real clue what they were looking for, let alone what they were doing. Ana had no real path; all she knew was she wanted to see the lights and buildings that her good friend Grace had told her about. She wanted to make a life that was her own. Grace had not oversold either. To Ana, Seattle is where she belonged. This is where she'd first found herself—away from her past.

At first, she and Haven had truly struggled, both of them working two to three jobs to afford rent. Before long, they were spending way more money on their lifestyle than their accommodation. A series of mistakes led them to consider moving back to Vancouver. Then, they met Anthony. Anthony was four years older, a semi-struggling artist from a wealthy family who had also run away to Seattle to make something of himself. He had been cut off from his family, having recently announced that he was gay, and went searching for acceptance. He had found it in the girls. He became best friends with Ana and Haven and enjoyed being able to share anything with them without fear of judgment. The three of them had a lot of fun together in the early days following their arrival in Seattle. There had been chaos, but they had also learned a lot about themselves and each other.

Their friends, who all sat around the table, had been picked up along the way, all of them looking for somewhere to belong. Ana looked around at them—they were a group of misfits who somehow managed to pull their life together to become the successes they were. Haven had found her calling in marketing. She'd started off as an assistant to a banking firm where she worked her way up, tirelessly juggling multiple projects until she got to where she was now: head of marketing for that same company who had taken her in as a sixteen-year-old glorified coffee maker.

Anthony had used his power of networking to get into the underground art scene, rubbing shoulders with other rich kids who had also been trying to make it as starving artists. They eventually introduced him to the right people. His art gallery had become extremely popular and was often where Ana and Haven started their Friday nights out, drinking at the bar with the big man himself as he updated them on his most recent show.

Then there was Anastasia Rose, the girl who thought she would not get far in life because many of the ones that loved her hurt her in ways that would never heal. The world had let her down, and the actions of betrayal she had endured made her feel unworthy. But Ana was a survivor. Little by little, she had been taking the steps that would one day lead her to decide that she was going to make something of herself, that she would prove to the world—and more importantly to herself—she *was* worthy of an amazing life no matter what had happened in her past. She no longer blamed herself for her grandfather's betrayal. Moving on from that shitty thing that happened to her as a young girl is what saved her and made her feel worthy again.

The stars had started to align in Ana's world to guide her to a new path, and while she hadn't known what she wanted to be, she did know she dreamed of being worlds away from who she had been. Once Anastasia learned how to become tough and confident, a company took notice of her. The world opened opportunities for her to go from a small-town Canadian girl into a fierce secret weapon in Corporate America. She was a true force to be reckoned with. She had bussed tables by day and schmoozed with the business elites by night, eventually landing a job in sales. Ana was guided by older friends who saw her determination and pushed her to make a name for herself. At twenty-six years old, she was making big money in the heart of Seattle and showed no signs of slowing down.

Ana was head of sales and had gotten close to the CEO of Global Communications, one of the biggest tech companies in Seattle. Life was good, and it only kept getting better. She was a world away from small-town Ana who had grown to become afraid of her own shadow. Now, Anastasia Rose rubbed shoulders with important people in business and had become their equal. People never questioned her right to sit at the VIP table, but sometimes Ana questioned whether anyone saw her insecurities. On those occasions, Haven would remind her of why they'd come to the city in the first place: "We can be anyone we want to be. Don't forget that you've earned your right to be anywhere you want and exactly where you are."

Of all the changes her life had gone through, Ana's relationship with her mother was one of the parts that never changed. No matter what she was going through or where she was, the one constant she had was her mom, who she often referred to as her "soulmate." They spoke several times a week. Nothing happened in Ana's life that her mother didn't know about. Then there was Haven. Together they had battled through traumas they'd only seen in movies. Yet here they were, seated around a table full of people who truly loved them and had been witness to their rise to success.

"Hey, don't tell me you're slowing down already!" Hilary, Ana's redheaded, loud-mouthed friend, laughed. She played the role of the hopeless romantic in their group. Hilary was coming out of her tenth relationship this year, and it was only April. Ana smiled and took her strawberry daiquiri from the table and chugged it. Tonight was a celebration, and she was going to enjoy every minute of it. Anthony ordered four bottles of champagne and Ana raised her eyebrow at him.

"What? We're celebrating!" He smiled, nudging Ana and once again raising his glass at her.

The group was in full party mode and was the loudest table in the restaurant. Ana excused herself to go to the bathroom. Her long black dress clung to her toned body as she made her way across the floor. She twirled her hair around her finger again, already feeling the buzz from the drinks. She thought about the business meeting she'd had this afternoon. She'd managed to secure a big client and her boss had praised her. The thought of having done a good job brought a smile to her face, and she wasn't paying as much attention as she should have been and bumped into somebody.

"Oh! I'm so sorry!" Ana said, leaning over to the man to help steady him.

"Hey! Watch where you're–" the man replied before looking at Ana and stopping mid-sentence. "Oh . . . I'm sorry. I didn't hurt you, did I?" His voice changed its tone and softened into concern. The way his brown eyes looked into Ana's made her blush, and she was thankful that the lights were dimmed so he wouldn't notice.

Handsome. Head to toe gorgeous. He was dressed in a tailored suit, smelled expensive, and had a soft, but gruff, voice. Ana felt herself weaken as he flashed her a smile.

"No . . . I . . . I didn't see you," she stammered, feeling herself blush more at the sudden onset of butterflies in her stomach. He let out a low seductive laugh as he realized she was still holding on to his elbow. Ana followed his eyes to where her hands were and let go quickly. Her blush deepened.

"It's not a problem. It's crowded in here." He kindly gave her an excuse.

Ana nodded. "Anyway, sorry again. I better, uh . . ." Ana apologized and gestured to the restroom, making her way around the gorgeous man who exuded sex and looked like he commanded any room he walked into just for being him. He straightened up and touched her shoulder gently. Her body shivered with excitement. *Get a grip on yourself, Ana,* she thought to herself.

"So soon?" he asked, his smile bringing tingles down Ana's spine. "Well . . . I hope I bump into you again." With that, he turned on his heel and walked back to his table. Ana watched as all eyes were on him. *He certainly commands a room* she thought to herself.

As Ana made her way out of the bathroom, she took a casual and quick glance in the direction of the handsome stranger's table, but it was now empty. She felt a pang of disappointment; she could have had a lot of fun with him. She adjusted her dress, carefully positioning the slit that accentuated her toned legs. She felt good and looked even better.

Making her way back to the table, she noticed that her group had grown in size. There were several people she didn't recognize sitting with her friends. Ana took her place in between Haven and Anthony. Anthony passed her a glass of champagne, his voice loud, showing just how drunk he had gotten since she'd been gone.

"And here is our other celebrant, Miss Anastasia Rose!" Ana smiled and looked around the table, a few new men and women smiled back at her, all strangers but one. Further down the table sat a newly familiar face that grinned back at her. Ana swallowed her excitement as she stared at the handsome stranger she'd just encountered.

Haven got up and hugged her friend, whispering in her ear, "Ana, Hilary pulled some hotties to our table. Which one's yours?" Ana giggled and pushed her friend away playfully, Ana rolled her eyes pretending to not want any part of the manhunt, deep down already knowing who she wanted. Hilary draped her arms around the handsome stranger, whispering something in his ear. Not once did he take his gaze away from Ana. She pretended not to notice as she got talking to the man opposite her. His name was Darren; he was tall, dark, handsome, and a rich banker. She could tell from the Rolex that proudly sat on his muscular wrist. Sure, he was charming. He seemed like a nice guy, but Ana twirled her hair around her finger and cut her eyes to the end of the table to see if the stranger was playing up to Hilary's attention. Hilary was still in his ear, and he seemed to be engrossed in their conversation. Ana felt a pang of jealousy. She knew that if Hilary wanted something, she got it. So Ana pushed herself to refocus on the conversation with Darren.

Her friends mingled. Anthony had found himself some eye candy. They had tucked themselves at the corner of the table, stealing kisses as if they were two teenagers. *Good for him,* Ana thought to herself. A little further down, Haven had moved to sit on a guy's lap and was in a full-blown make-out session as if no one else was around. Her other friends were talking, laughing, and drinking with other people. Darren had started to bore her with bad finance jokes. Ana was not overly picky when it came to hookups, but tonight she wanted more intelligent conversation. She had a whole bottle of champagne to herself and used it to divert herself while Darren talked about his career and his love for horses. Ana couldn't relate and introduced him to her friend, Sienna, who had been caught in a debate with a few other people. Sienna looked at her, thankful that she had been pulled out of the conversation. They seemed to hit it off right away. Ana smiled as she felt she had managed to dodge the most boring bullet in town.

Getting up, Ana made her way to the bar. If she was going to get through the orgy that her friends had started forming, she needed to get drunk. As she waited to be served, a hand suddenly rested at the small of her back. She felt a familiar tingle on her exposed skin as she looked beside her to find the handsome stranger.

"What's your poison?" he asked, totally oblivious to what his touch had done to her.

"Actually, I think I'm ready for shots." She smiled.

"That bad, huh?" He laughed, flashing his beautiful, perfect teeth at her. Ana felt her knees give a little as she looked away. Why did he have that effect on her?

"I'm Ana by the way," she said, putting her hand out to him.

"Hunter," he replied, taking her delicate hands into his and kissing it gently. She was not expecting it and couldn't help but think about how soft his lips were against her hand. Her body stiffened. He was not going to be good for her, she knew it, but at that moment, she couldn't think of anything other than feeling his body on hers.

They took a few shots together and then joined their friends who had migrated to the dance floor. Was it just Ana's imagination, or did the music get louder? The bar got hotter as she danced with her friends. Hunter was never too far away. Hilary had found herself back at his side, dancing seductively. This time, Ana was jealous. Guilt followed soon after as the one thing she never wanted was the drama of fighting over a guy with one of her friends. Haven and Anthony were whispering between themselves, and Ana looked at them both wanting to be part of their conversation.

"We were just saying how embarrassing Hilary is being," Haven said a little too loudly as her drunk voice took over her ability to whisper. Anthony nodded, sipping his martini and dancing to the music. Ana rolled her eyes again. She was above gossiping, and yet she couldn't help but feel some kind of triumph. As Hilary ground against Hunter, he looked up and locked eyes with Ana. He rolled his eyes, which made Ana giggle quietly to herself.

Haven tugged at Ana as Anthony used Haven to balance himself. "He's into you, you know?" Haven raised an eyebrow at Ana. How was it that even in her state of mind Haven could still read a room perfectly?

Anthony nodded. "Go get what's yours!" he said as his unexpected companion grabbed him from behind and the two of them excused themselves off the dance floor. Haven winked at Ana, pushing her a little closer to Hunter, and then went off to find her new friend. Hunter watched as Ana made her way toward him while Hilary still danced, performing for Hunter.

"Hey, Hil. I saw the guy from the other day at the bar," Ana said, knowing it would lead her friend to go and hunt down the guy who had escaped her clutches. Hilary stopped dancing, her face looking serious as she made a beeline toward the bar. Hunter pretended to sigh with relief and pulled Ana immediately toward him, holding her ever so lightly by the small of her back. *My god, he smelled good*, Ana thought to herself.

"I never thought she'd leave, so thank you," he whispered into her ear, his lips touching her skin softly. Ana moaned internally.

"Tell me. What was it about Hilary that enticed you?" Ana asked cheekily, wanting to play a little with Hunter, knowing it may be a dangerous thing to do. Her body knew what it wanted.

Hunter looked at her, surprised by her question. "What makes you think I was interested *in her*?" Ana knew immediately from the way he said the words and pressed into her body that he wanted her just as much as she wanted him. With Hillary out of the way, she could take her turn to dance with him, and wow, could he move.

Within moments, it felt like they were the only ones there, and the music took over. The heat radiated between them. Sweat glided down their skin, making them hotter than they should be, but their bodies moved in sync together. The short, ragged breaths indicated the lust between them was palpable.

The scent of his aftershave mixed with their sweat made her want him even more. Hunter grabbed Ana's face with both hands and drove his tongue deep into her mouth. She had wanted to taste him and was pleased that he seemed to feel the same. Unable to help herself, she grabbed his hair and pulled him closer to her, eager to taste more of him. In her mind, she knew something about Hunter was dangerous, but none of that mattered at that moment. She wanted him, and he definitely wanted her. The aching tension between them built up to a point where neither could stand it anymore.

Still fully in control, Hunter whispered everything their bodies were saying. "I want you now." Hunter's words breached her defenses. With those four words, they were gone.

* * *

Ana got ready for work Monday morning and couldn't help thinking about her night with Hunter. What she liked the most was that she found someone on her level when it came to intelligence and wit. Hunter was her kind of man: confident, a gentleman in public, and a completely different story behind closed doors. If truth be told, Ana knew nothing about him. She did Google him the next day, finding him in plenty of photos with gorgeous women. One article even referred to him as the "Sexiest Bachelor in Seattle." When she saw that, Ana felt she shouldn't hold out hope. But the way he hungrily took her body in, kissing every part of her skin, made her feel like she had never felt before. She could still smell his cologne on her body.

Ana shivered as she remembered how he had undressed her. He was gentle at first, taking in every moment as she'd held her breath, letting him explore her. Her impatient hands had tugged at his shirt, untying each button in eagerness to see more of his chiseled body. Every undone button caused her body to ache even more. She pulled him closer to her until they were skin to skin. As they kissed, she found herself carried away by a fantasy she didn't even want to acknowledge to herself, but she pretended anyway. After all, this was a game Anastasia was good at. She imagined Hunter thinking about how she was a stunningly beautiful woman, perfect in every way: her body, her mind, her skin. She imagined him thinking they were a match for each other in every sense. She imagined him wanting her more than he's ever wanted anybody else. Ana caught herself thinking this again and internally chastised herself. *Men who felt like that didn't exist,* she thought. Secretly, it's why she never exchanged phone numbers, so that they couldn't break the fantasy she'd created. and this way, she couldn't be betrayed by anyone *again.*

She was still flushed from her memories when she walked into the boardroom.

"So, Ana, what magic did you use to win the Harvey account?" teased her colleague, Piper, from across the room. Ana helped herself to coffee before taking her seat at the table.

"No magic. Just charm." Ana winked, causing Piper to giggle. Ana loved Monday mornings. She and Piper were always first to the board meeting, which meant they could gossip about what happened over the weekend and have all the womanly chats they couldn't have in front of their team which was mostly men. Piper shared her ups and downs of being married to her childhood sweetheart.

Ana loved to hear her stories because they often restored her faith in men, leading her to believe some men truly loved without inflicting betrayal. Piper often told Ana that love was a decision to be committed to one another faithfully, especially through the hard times. She remembered one particular time when Piper had said, "Loving someone during the fun times is easy but it's the willingness to support and love each other through life's hardest hurdles, that is what truly makes or breaks a marriage." Ana could tell how much Piper loved her husband. Ana secretly hoped she could one day find this type of love too. But she often asked herself and her therapist if she was worthy of that kind of love. After years of therapy, Ana was aware that this kind of thinking was toxic, but she saved all those thoughts for her journals where she let all her true feelings out, the ones that haunted her deep inside her soul. She often thought of it as the other Ana, the person no one knew—the Ana that hid behind a mask. Ana had spent countless hours trying to reconcile her feelings in her journals. The thoughts would circle in her head until she felt she had some clarity, but they'd often come back after conversations with Piper.

Ana filled Piper in on her night with Hunter and how they had spent their Saturday barely seeing the sunlight.

"So will you see him again?" Piper asked, completely engrossed in Ana's story. She lived her "single life" vicariously through Ana and loved the dirty updates her colleague had for her.

"Never!" Ana shook her head "We didn't even exchange numbers. It was just a hookup." Ana laughed, secretly feeling a pang of disappointment in her stomach. She was used to one-night stands, but that didn't stop her from sometimes wishing someone would stay and want more.

"Seems like he put out good at least." Piper laughed, shuffling her papers. Ana stirred herself into business mode as their colleagues filed into the boardroom.

Their meeting went as any Monday did. There were the typical boys' club jokes that went over Ana and Piper's heads. They sat pretty, which was what they were hired for, but Ana knew she was capable of more than just being eye candy for the sex-starved older men in her office. That's what made her a secret weapon. For years, Ana had used her looks to convince powerful men into letting her into their meetings. She listened and then took the knowledge she gained to teach herself how to be just as powerful, cleverer, and hungrier than any of the men that had years and experience above her.

Mr. Jacobson, the CEO, favored Ana. Everyone in the boardroom knew that. He thought the world of her because of how hard she worked. Her hard work showed in the kinds of clients she was pulling in. Everyone in the office fought for Mr. Jacobson's approval, but jealousy often focused on Ana. At first, this intimidated her. She'd have to constantly remind herself that she belonged there and worked hard to have a seat at the executive table. She worked harder than anyone else because she was an ambitious woman with many dreams to fulfill. She knew that meant she had to work harder than anyone in the room.

Mr. Jacobson had built his company from humble beginnings. He appreciated hard work much more than brownnosing, which is what drew him to Ana. In his old age, he took much more of a backseat than he had wanted to, but even he could admit it was of some relief to him. But still, no matter what, he always made it to the Monday meetings to make sure he was still involved in everything. If he had complete control, he would put Ana in a much higher position than she was now. He once told her that he would have loved to be able to train her to take over someday, but The Old Boys Club that filled his office would never allow it. Instead, he did what he could to equip Ana with every opportunity to feed her hunger to learn more.

As the meeting—a meeting that could have been an email—ended, and before his team could get up from their chairs, he cleared his throat.

"I'd like to say well done to Anastasia." He stood and gestured to her, making the table look at Ana who was midway through drinking her coffee. Ana smiled awkwardly at Mr. Jacobson.

"Through sheer hard work and determination, Anastasia managed to finally convince Harvey Estates to sign a contract with us," he announced, beaming at his young protégé. Her colleagues congratulated Ana and celebrated her achievement with handshakes and pats on the back. Ana knew a lot of it was for show, and though she deserved to be celebrated, she would surely be on the back end of quite a few jealous comments and jokes later on from her colleagues who had spent years trying to secure the same client with no success.

Ana got up to leave the boardroom when Mr. Jacobson called her back in.

"Anastasia, you know Mrs. Jacobson and I don't enjoy nights out much anymore. We were invited to a party, and I thought perhaps you could have our tickets. Maybe you and a couple of friends could go? I'm sure you'd have much more fun than we would." He didn't wait for Ana to respond before handing her three tickets.

"Thank you, sir." He walked away, leaving Ana staring at the invitations, unsure what to do with them. By the way they glittered and their sheer weight, Ana knew this was an exclusive party. She got back to her office and immediately texted Anthony and Haven and told them about the party. In typical Haven fashion, the response came quickly. Anthony's response followed shortly after.

Both were in. All that was left was for them to find outfits for their first masquerade ball.

* * *

Stepping out of the black car, Anthony straightened his suit and put his mask on, turning to help the ladies out of the car. Haven stepped out first, adjusting the straps on her emerald gown. She carefully placed her mask on her face. Anthony escorted Ana out of the car. All eyes instantly found her. She was radiant in a beautiful, silver ball gown that grazed the floor and was accessorized with the most stunning diamonds. The back of her dress dipped so low you could see the small of the back and her soft, smooth skin. Her dress made her feel like a princess as it billowed out around her. Her long hair framed her petite body with the slightest of curls. A stunning mask glittered as it covered the top half of her face, adorned with an intricate design that matched her gown. She made sure she felt just as beautiful on the inside as she did on the outside. Anthony proudly escorted both his friends, one on each arm. Cameras were flashing constantly as they exited the car.

Ana could feel the wealth and luxury oozing from every corner of the room. A big band played on a beautiful stage. Gloved waiters stood against the walls while others passed trays of food that Ana doubted she could pronounce. Chandeliers glittered like the diamonds and gems on the wrists and necks of the women around her. She could easily picture herself in a life where this was the norm.

The grand entrance glowed with golden lights as if the gates into heaven just opened with gold chandeliers that spiraled down the walls, illuminating the glimmering golden walls; the floor was polished so brightly that it looked like an iced-over lake. It was not just the ballroom that was spectacular; it was also the women. They sparkled like a box of diamonds in shades of ruby, emerald, and amethysts, all swirling before them. Low murmurs of their chatter accompanied a room filled with large blooms of oriental lilies and roses, covering the space with their beautiful color and smell. The room was nothing short of breathtaking.

The whole event screamed opulence. "We're not in Kansas anymore . . ." marveled Haven, causing her two friends to laugh quietly to themselves. Champagne was being poured by the most elegant servers Ana had ever seen. *So this is how the other half lived*, she thought to herself. Guests dressed head to toe in designer dress wear; the price tags would cause even the biggest shopaholic to shed a tear. Ana felt slight discomfort. Moments like these, surrounded by Seattle's elite—the wealthy world of old money, powerful CEOs, and billion-dollar bank accounts—normally would have reminded her of where she had come from. But tonight, Anastasia stole the show in every way. From the moment she walked in, all eyes were on her, and she reveled in the attention, knowing full well she worked hard to get there. And she did belong. Ana was damn good at what she did, and she always did it with integrity and honesty. There would be no negative talk tonight.

"How do you guys like it?" Ana asked, trying to mask her nerves. Anthony stood speechless as he tried to take in the view. Grand would not even come close to how everything looked. From top to bottom, the ballroom screamed decadence.

The friends were escorted to their table to set their things down. They were seated with friends of Mr. and Mrs. Jacobson, who welcomingly introduced themselves. The table got to know each other, exchanging information about themselves. "Anastasia, Duncan always talks very fondly of you. He says you are fantastic at your work!" A lady, who had introduced herself as the wife of Mr. Jacobson's best friend, exclaimed. She looked radiant in her ruby-studded dress and with her long flowing red hair.

"Thank you, Mrs. Reese," Ana replied politely. "Mr. Jacobson is a great mentor and boss. He's great inspiration to work hard."

A few glasses of champagne later, the entertainment had begun. There was so much going on that the three decided to circle the ballroom to get a view of everything.

People had already gotten up and started dancing. Some men had excused themselves to the smoking room to smoke cigars. Anthony was already drawn to a few men who had caught his eye, mainly one who had made his way to the smoking room.

"Can we head to the smoking room? I spy someone intriguing." Anthony was already plotting.

"Sure." Ana shrugged and agreed but was interrupted by Haven.

"Guys! We can't yet. This is the perfect opportunity for me to finally land a rich husband. I need you as my wing people." Despite this being an ongoing joke, Haven meant exactly what she said.

This was part of the fun of being able to attend parties like these. They had the opportunity to meet the elites they never got the chance to meet. On a few occasions, Ana found herself introducing herself to strangers who would make a point of telling her how beautiful she looked. She kept reminding herself that she was here under the invitation of Mr. Jacobson and therefore was to be on her best behavior. Anthony and Haven had already forgotten where they were and were lapping up the champagne that flowed so freely.

Haven was involved with a man dressed in a black silk tuxedo, who in her words "smelled rich," so Ana and Anthony excused themselves to make their way to the dance floor.

"Since when did everyone become professional ballroom dancers?" Ana asked. Anthony marveled at the skills of those around them.

Anthony laughed. "Us old money folks, we're taught how to dance in a way that will make everyone else feel poor." He laughed. Ana adjusted her mask and watched in awe of everyone who seemed to dance so elegantly and with ease.

Anthony, knowing Ana the way he did, took her hand and said, "I got you, baby girl." He smiled reassuringly at his best friend as he guided her through the dance, gliding together along the floor. Ana felt light and delicate in his arms. Feeling more comfortable with herself, Ana allowed herself to enjoy the moment under the sparkling chandelier to the beautiful tune of the piano and string orchestra. It felt like she was in a movie. "If only my mom could see me right now!" she said to Anthony as she giggled.

Anthony did a great job at making Ana look like a professional dancer too. She felt less out of place and more like she belonged there. Haven waved from the side of the dance floor, beckoning them over to her. They rolled their eyes but gracefully made their way over to her through the dancers.

"Cameron is going to the smoking room as he wants to talk to someone about business," she whispered to her friends. Ana laughed. This meant she wanted her wing friends to come with her.

Ana had expected the room to be as it was back when she was an underage teen. She waited to start choking from the smoke as they went through the doors, but instead, she was met with what could only be described as the most elegant library she had ever seen. The dark paneled walls and expensive furnishings are what she imagined an old gentleman's quarters must have looked like. Rightfully so, as most of the guests there were old men in expensive suits holding cigars. Anthony was offered his own cigar upon entry, which he gladly took, and Ana reached her hand out to take one too. Haven made her way to her new companion Cameron, quickly forgetting her nerves. Anthony spotted the guy he had seen earlier, and he and Ana made their way over to him.

Ana and Anthony introduced themselves. Anthony's eye candy introduced himself as Ian Winthorp Jr. His parents were the hosts of the masquerade ball and, from the sounds of it, were very important people. A few others introduced themselves, but it was clear to Ana that Anthony and Ian had eyes only for each other. Exchanging coy smiles while talking about how fabulous the party was, Ana watched as her friend showed unusual signs of being shy. Being a welcoming host, Ian ensured everyone felt comfortable, all the while getting closer to Anthony. Ian made every excuse to speak to him directly and brush his arm against Anthony's. Ana watched like it was her favorite TV show, rooting for Anthony to have the romance he dreamed of. A new group of guests came into the room. Ian spotted a friend of his and beckoned him over. Ana's body stiffened as she smelled the delicious familiar scent of aftershave. Pretending not to have noticed, she waited to be introduced.

"Hunter, these are my new friends, Anthony and Ana." Hunter's gaze fell on Ana instantly. His mouth dropped slightly before he quickly composed himself.

"Pleased to meet you both," he said, his bright blue eyes shining through his silk black mask, eyes that would forever be etched into her brain. She knew it was him, and he clearly knew it was her. Ana blushed; the room immediately started to feel hotter. The spark between them couldn't be ignored, but they were at a ball. *Maybe this was the opportunity to actually get to know a little about this mysterious man*, thought Ana.

Conversation flowed as they spoke about work. Hunter admitted hearing Ana's name pop up in conversation within the business world.

"You've made some very powerful fans, Ana," Hunter said in an approving tone.

"Oh, so it's Ana that you've been looking for all night, H?" Ian asked, causing Hunter to smile smugly.

"Well, I didn't know it was this Ana," he replied, nodding to the confused Ana.

"You were looking for me?" she asked, looking from Ian to Hunter as she waited for an explanation.

"Hunter's boss asked him to meet the wildfire, Ana, they'd been hearing so much about," Ian explained.

"He wanted me to find out what it would take for you to join us in our firm," Hunter continued. Surprise didn't describe the gravity of how Ana felt at that moment. She knew she was good at her job, but to be headhunted at such an extravagant party seemed too good to be true.

"You're kidding, right?" Ana blurted, unable to contain her disbelief. Anthony laughed and nudged Ana.

"People are finally talking about your amazing skills, Ana," he said encouragingly.

"I don't understand . . ." Ana began, stopping mid-sentence to absorb what Hunter was offering her.

"Perhaps you'd allow me a few minutes of your time to explain? Maybe somewhere a little more private?" Hunter put his arm out for Ana to take. Ian looked at Anthony longingly and, without hesitating, insisted Hunter and Ana leave to have their conversation. Ana kissed Anthony on the cheek and thanked Ian for his hospitality before following Hunter. Hunter led Ana through the dance floor. People parted to make way for him. Before she could think about why that may be, someone bumped into Ana, knocking her over. Hunter's strong arms immediately grabbed her whole body before she fell in embarrassment to the floor. Ana looked up as

Hunter held her in his arms. They were so close they could kiss. Ana looked at Hunter, shocked and slightly embarrassed. But the look on Hunter's face was a heated one. He quickly swooped her up and offered his arm, continuing to casually walk through the rest of the dance floor, never letting Ana go. Her heart fluttered in her chest. Hunter's face didn't give anything away. Ana hoped that was because he was serious about one thing: getting out of the ballroom with Ana. They exited the dance floor through a gap within the white silk curtains draping the walls. Pushing them aside slightly, he exposed a glass door leading to a balcony. Lit up with magnificent twinkling lights, it looked like they were walking on a floor of stars.

They made their way to the end of the balcony that overlooked the ocean. Ana inhaled the sea air and took in the magic of the night. It felt like a fairy tale. She knew it would eventually end, since fairy tales always ended with a happily ever after and conveniently forget what happens next. But she was determined to embrace the moment without letting the inevitable fear of betrayal creep in.

"So, tell me, was this an elaborate joke to get me alone out here?" Ana asked cheekily, wishing they could have a repeat of their first night together while also hoping there truly was a dream job offer for her.

Hunter laughed and put his arms around Ana's petite waist. "Okay, business first, I suppose." He stepped back from her but kept his hands around her.

"There's a new department opening in the company. Starling Enterprises. Heard of it?"

Ana's mouth dropped. Starling Enterprises was a multibillion-dollar company and one of the biggest in the city. *They'd heard of her?*

Ana shook her head in disbelief and closed her mouth. "And what, you want me to . . .?"

"I want you to come and join us as our head of sales."

Ana raised her lips in a half-smile. She didn't want to sound ungrateful, but she felt a slight disappointment. She looked down at her hands. She'd been head of sales for a good part of three years, and she was ready to progress.

"You're already head of sales, I know, but this comes with a lot of benefits and a pretty hefty pay increase."

Ana thought about what this might mean for her career and her future. She was being held back from any kind of advancement by The Old Boys Club, and this might give her more of a ladder to climb in a huge international company.

"I'd like to think about it," Ana told him. Hunter's smile never once wavered from his face as he pulled Ana closer to him.

"Can we move past the business, then?" He kissed her lips tenderly before wordlessly unleashing what was really on his mind. His hands hungrily explored her body. She hesitated, looking behind him to see if anyone was coming.

Hunter laughed. "Relax. No one will come out here. They're all too busy being wowed by everything going on inside."

Ana looked at him, surprised. He seemed used to this. She was not a prude, but she already felt out of place. Being caught having sex on a balcony at the fanciest party she had ever been to would definitely make her feel uncomfortable.

Hunter pulled away from Ana, sensing her discomfort. He took her hand and leaned against the balcony. Ana apologized and touched his face with her gloved hand. She stroked the back of his neck, causing him to groan.

"I just wanted to relive the other night," he explained with a desire in his eyes that she had never seen before, it was as if he was hungry for *her*. He pulled Ana up against him. She could feel his arousal, and it caused her body to tighten in excitement. His hands gripped her body as they locked lips, tongues intertwining. The lingering taste of mint in his mouth met her tongue. The smell of his aftershave that continuously invaded her dreams impaled her senses. His lips were warm and soft against hers. Boldly, Ana reached down, discreetly unzipping his pants as he lifted her gown. Lifting Ana up, he perched her against the edge of the balcony. Ana moaned as he kissed her neck tenderly. She moved her hands down his length as he pulled down her lace underwear. He groaned as he kissed her again and then thrust inside of her. Ana bit her lip, suppressing the urge to moan at the pleasure she felt. He moved inside of her amidst the twinkling lights surrounding them on the balcony, her pleasure building. She hoped this fairy tale would never end.

Chapter 9

Two weeks later, the pretty blonde receptionist at Starling Enterprises called up to the main office while Ana straightened her suit. Sneaking a glance at herself in the mirror behind the reception desk, she tucked a stray strand of hair behind her ear. She felt confident and ready to start her first day at Starling Enterprises. She wanted to make a good impression. It had been a long time since she was the new girl, and her nerves had woken her up way too early. She had not seen Hunter since the night they made love at the masquerade ball and wondered whether she would see him today. After accepting his offer, she had been contacted by a man named Zack Haskell, who would be her manager, and the rest was history. Mr. Jacobson had been disappointed to lose her but understood her reasons for wanting to leave. He couldn't compete with the package Starling was offering her. She sighed a little, thinking of how much she owed him for her work experiences while she waited to be called up to Zack's office. She steadied her shaking hand. *Calm down, Anastasia Rose. You've got this*, she thought to herself, trying to muster the nerves of steel she worked so hard to develop over the years.

"Ana?" Another pretty blonde woman approached her. Beautiful and tall, she looked more like a model than someone who worked in an office. "Hi! My name is Clara. I'm Mr. Haskell's assistant. Are you ready to come up?" She smiled and led Ana to the elevator.

Ana stepped into a busy office with towering ceilings, top to bottom glass windows, all-white furniture, and a breathtaking view of Seattle. Ana took a deep breath and looked around. A few faces turned to watch as they made their way to Zack Haskell's office. Clara opened the door as Ana followed her. Sitting behind a large oak desk was a tanned, handsome man dressed in a crisp suit. A wide smile greeted her.

"Anastasia!" He beamed, getting up from his desk to shake her hand.

"Mr. Haskell. So lovely to finally meet you." She smiled back.

"Please, call me Zack." He thanked Clara and asked that she join them on Ana's tour of the office.

Her first day was filled with a meet and greet of the various teams within the large hub. With so many faces, titles, and roles, Ana started to feel overwhelmed, and wanted to hide behind one of the many masks she'd cultivated for herself in times of stress. Finally, she was called into a working lunch. A delicious spread was laid out. People had already taken their seats when Ana walked in. Ana sat beside a gentleman with glasses and brown curly hair. He introduced himself as Alexander Jenkins, the lead business analyst in their department.

Ana couldn't help but notice how intelligent he was, despite showing his nervousness. His striking green eyes sparkled as he talked about his work. Normally, if a guy at a bar talked the same way he did, she would assume they were bragging, but in Alexander, she could see his genuine passion for what he did. Sure, he was a little bit nerdy, but Ana couldn't help but be attracted to his work ethic and intelligence. He asked Ana about her work history. Ana subtlety guided the conversation toward topics outside of the workplace as she found herself wanting to get to know him more. During their brief conversation, she found out he was an only child as his parents had passed away, but he was played tennis regularly as his form of therapy. Ana, in turn, shared she had recently celebrated her tenth anniversary of living in Seattle. Alexander congratulated her.

Alexander introduced Ana to several of their other colleagues. Slowly, her nerves began to ease. Alexander had a calming effect on Ana, who felt like she was experiencing her first day of school. Though, she could also say that she felt like some kind of museum exhibit since most of her colleagues had already heard of her and were curious about her; she had made quite the impression on some bosses higher up, and gossip had been rife, saying that the talented Anastasia Rose would be joining them.

"Now here I am." Ana laughed, making her colleagues join in her laughter. Lunch went quickly, and everyone soon started filing out. Alexander was back at her side chatting away. Ana couldn't help but feel like they had been friends forever.

"Thanks, Alexander," Ana said, touching his arm gently.

"For what?" he asked, confused.

"It's never easy being the new person in the office. Thanks for making my first lunch less nerve-wracking." She smiled at him.

"What? Confident Anastasia was feeling nervous?" He raised his eyebrows, surprised. Ana burst out laughing and pushed him playfully.

"Still, thanks." She smiled. "It was really great to meet you." Ana put out her hand and Alexander took it, shaking it firmly. His touch electrified Ana. It felt warm and tender. Alexander held on a second longer than she was expecting. Did she imagine it, or did he squeeze a little tighter than people normally do? Alexander grinned at Ana and waved goodbye to her as he walked back to his office. Ana watched as he walked away. She had to be careful, first Hunter, then potentially Alexander? But still.

There was something different about him, and she couldn't wait to get to know more.

* * *

The weeks flew by in her new environment, especially without the added distraction of Hunter. There was more work than she could handle, and Ana often found herself relaxing at lunch with Alexander and his soft smile. Within a few months, she had impressed her bosses so much that she was invited to attend her first work event. She was dressed to impress in her tight red dress that showcased her enviable figure, her hair up in a sleek chignon.

Ana checked herself in the mirror as she walked into the cocktail bar, reminding herself that she belonged at this event. Ana was greeted by Zack and was quickly introduced to who she assumed were very important people in Starling Enterprises. They complimented the work she had been doing. In her short time there, she had already led them through some big partnerships, securing noteworthy clients, including her previous company: Global Communications. She was managing accounts that were worth millions of dollars and making profits worth praising. Ana politely smiled and thanked them before being pulled away by Zack to mingle with other guests.

Ana turned to follow Zack. She smelled him before she saw him. Hunter was there. A moment later, their eyes locked, and their desire for each other was undeniable, even from across the room. Ana hoped no one else could feel what she felt. Much like a moth to a light, his piercing blue eyes locked onto hers, and with slight amusement etched on his face, he started to make his way over to their group.

"Hello, Anastasia," he breathed close to her ear as he nodded politely to the other guests. Hunter had been in London for business, and though their relationship was not something she could label, Ana had missed seeing his face in the office and, if she was honest with herself, in the bedroom.

As a director for Starling, Hunter was good at playing pretenses. Did he know how much she longed for him as he led meetings? Was he aware that she couldn't stop undressing him in her imagination whenever he showed his power in the boardroom? Ana both admired and was intimidated by him. Sometimes she liked to show him how good she was too, flaunting her successes in the short space of time she had been there. She always had to remind herself he had seniority over her, as well as the fact that they were not officially together. That fact caused her some jealousy whenever she witnessed the women in the office flirt with him. She would never admit it, but more than a time or two, she would allow herself to take out her jealousy and anger with him in the bedroom. Not that he ever complained. In fact, he always enjoyed it when she took control.

Hunter pulled Ana away from the group and led her to the bar. They ordered their drinks and stood in silence for a few moments.

"How was your trip?" Ana felt compelled to be near him but also didn't want to give away the annoyance she felt. He had been back from London for a week now, which she's had to hear through the grapevine in the office. He hadn't called or texted her directly. Hunter flashed her his deliciously gorgeous smile. Sheepishly, he touched her face and sighed. Ana closed her eyes, taking in his aroma: aftershave and alcohol. She couldn't resist his allure; he made her weak in the knees.

"I missed touching you," he whispered, letting his lips touch her bare shoulder, sending electricity through her skin.

"Prove it." Ana let her mouth fall into a slight smile as he looked expectantly at her. Hunter turned to discreetly walk away. Ana waited for a few seconds before following him, careful not to draw too much attention.

Out of sight, Hunter took Ana's hand into his and led her down the grand hallway. Turning to the left, he opened a door and led Ana in. Ana was surprised to see them in a bathroom. It was fancy, yes, but a bathroom, nonetheless. Ana turned to face Hunter as he smiled cheekily. "Really?" Ana raised an eyebrow.

"Really." He pulled Ana close to him and reached behind her, unzipping the back of her dress. She pulled his tuxedo jacket off, then moved to unbutton his shirt. Naked, she stood in front of him in only her six-inch stilettos. Hunter looked up and down, his eyes taking in every inch of her. Ana happily allowed him to drink her in, enjoying his appreciation for her body. Ana knelt in front of him. Now it was her turn to show him how much she appreciated him.

* * *

Ana giggled into Hunter's shoulder as they tried to sneak out of the bathroom unnoticed. Once they got closer to the main bar, Ana pulled away and walked ahead of him. As soon as she got into the room, her eyes met Zack's. He smiled and waved her over. He was in the middle of a conversation with a few other people she recognized from one of their many meetings. Zack introduced her and Ana smiled politely, engrossing herself in the conversation. She looked up, scanning the crowd to see if Hunter had entered yet, but she couldn't see him.

It was midnight when Ana realized she was on the verge of getting drunk. Her exhaustion wanted her to call it a night. She always believed you shouldn't get drunk at a work event, even if everyone else did. She knew the rumors that would follow her if she wasn't careful with her drinks or her sex life.

Before she left, she looked for Zack to thank him for helping her navigate her first work event. The evening had given her a better grasp of the importance of networking, especially when it came to succeeding in her role. It was not the worst thing either having access to an open bar and a chance to get dressed up. And all as part of her work? It still felt surreal.

As she scanned the room for her boss, she saw Hunter at the bar. He was standing with a pretty blonde and the two seemed in deep conversation. Ana felt a pang of jealousy. She reminded herself that Hunter was an important man who was often talking to all sorts of women. He would never dare flirt with someone else, especially not so soon after their encounter in the bathroom. *Would he?* Ana tried to shake her worries. She was sure it was all innocent, so she started making her way over to them. Part of her was trying to convince herself that her only intention was to say bye to him. Deep down, however, she knew she was trying to find out if it was truly innocent.

As she got closer, she saw the woman pull at Hunter's shirt and press her lips against his. His lips where Ana's had been only a few hours before. Lips that had touched every inch of Ana's skin. Ana felt a knot in her stomach, and she stopped in her tracks. At that moment, Hunter's eyes found hers. Ana felt tears prickle her eyes. Hunter said something to his companion as Ana turned on her heels and exited the party.

* * *

Ana sat at her desk, staring into space. It had been a long week with working extra hours to complete a project for one of her largest clients. The silence of the office was driving her insane. It had been a busy couple of days, and she had no doubt everyone had been wanting some peace and quiet to de-stress. Ana had been working so hard that she had no time to think about the networking event she had been to, which meant she had no time to analyze Hunter's behavior. Ana sighed and felt the threat of tears sting her eyes. She had allowed herself to cry only one time—over ice cream with Haven and Anthony, both of whom were having surprising luck with their partners. Since the event, Ana promised herself not to allow herself to be fooled again, choosing to ignore the many calls and messages Hunter had sent her. Ignoring him in the office was not easy; he was her superior. But then again, he had not been in much, and she'd managed to get away with making excuses to skip meetings she knew he would be in. She also made it a point to avoid the elevator and take the stairs in their high-rise office. Her quads and calves had been miserable, but it had been worth it to avoid him.

"Ana?" called a friendly voice behind her.

Ana looked up to be greeted with Alexander holding two coffees. "Hazelnut latte, right?" he asked, handing her one of the mugs.

Caught off guard, Ana took it and threw him a surprised look. "Thanks, Alexander," she started, but he put his hand up and shook it.

"It's nothing. I just noticed you looking a little down lately." Ana's heart warmed. Alexander was a goofy guy, offering plenty of laugh-out-loud moments. He was so caring toward her. On the many occasions where she'd forget to bring an umbrella with her, he would come along as her knight in shining armor to give her his. She probably had five of his umbrellas at her house at this point. Ana looked fondly at Alexander as he made it his mission to bring a smile back on her face. He really was the kind of person her mother would be happy for her to bring home. He was just so easy-going and fun to talk to. Much like Ana, he seemed to have a sense of darkness wash over him whenever she asked questions about his past. He was carefree, lived for the moment. Ana liked that about him, though sometimes he would seem a little reckless, never really thinking much into the future. The complete opposite, Ana had spent the last five years of her life only living for the future. Perhaps that is why she was so drawn to Alexander. He was fun, spontaneous, never really serious. He reminded Ana to be present.

Harper, Ana's colleague who had quickly become her right-hand woman, approached the two holding a large bunch of flowers.

"Someone's lucky!" Ana grinned, eyeing up the elaborate bouquet.

"They're not for me!" Harper smiled.

"For me?" Alexander gasped, dramatically reaching for the flowers. Harper and Ana laughed as Harper placed the flowers on Ana's desk before grabbing a seat and turning to the other two. Ana opened the card. There was only a short message written on it: "I'm sorry. Please forgive me." Harper raised one of her carefully shaped eyebrows. "Is it from who I think it is?" she asked coyly. Ana nodded. Having worked extremely close together over the past few months, Harper had slowly become Ana's trusted confidant. The two ladies shared their taste in expensive liquor and bad men.

Without realizing it, Alexander let out a loud breath of air. His brows furrowed as he looked at the flowers. Slowly, he got up from his perch on Ana's desk and excused himself. Harper's eyes followed him before looking back at Ana.

"So?" she asked expectantly.

"So what?" Ana teased.

Harper sighed. Before Ana could reply, she saw Hunter walking toward them. Ana straightened up.

"Hello, Ana . . . Harper." Hunter nodded to the two ladies. "Ana . . . may I speak to you for a moment?" Hunter's voice was cool and low, causing Ana's heart to do somersaults. She hid her emotions and felt her walls build up with cold indifference as she looked at Hunter.

"Sorry, Harper and I are in the middle of a really important meeting right now," Ana replied.

Hunter nodded. "Perhaps later," he said before excusing himself. Harper looked at Ana.

"Oh girl, you're torturing him." She laughed before Ana threw out a fake laugh too. Inside, she felt rattled. Did she really reject him to his face?

"Anyway, we're still on for tonight, right? I need a few drinks." Harper pleaded. Ana laughed again before agreeing to meet her at the lobby after work.

Ana pushed Hunter out of her mind and got back to work. Before long, she realized she'd been at it nonstop for several hours. Wanting to stretch her legs and get away from her computer, Ana went to get herself another coffee. She stopped by Alexander's office to ask him if he wanted to join her. His eyes lit up as he got up.

"I was looking for an excuse to take a walk anyway." He grinned. "Want to grab a snack in the cafeteria?"

Ana hadn't realized how hungry she was. Maybe something more than coffee would be a good idea. "Lead the way."

As they walked, Alexander told a dramatic story of his tennis match over the weekend. His facial expressions and impersonation of his seemingly drunk competition made Ana laugh loudly. She clutched at her sides as she gasped for breath. Laughing so hard at his story, Ana grabbed Alexander's arms, which encouraged him to continue performing. Ana had not laughed like this in so long. Alexander had a wonderful way of making her feel childish and ... happy.

"Anastasia?" called a familiar voice behind them. Alexander and Ana turned around to see Hunter walking up to them. "Can I have a word with you in my office?

Now, please?" Hunter insisted. He said it as if it were an invitation, but his tone told Ana she needed to accept it.

Ana nodded. There was no one to rescue her from whatever this was. She turned to Alexander. "You go on ahead. I'll meet you there."

Ana trailed behind him to his office. When his office door closed, Hunter didn't let down his steely composure.

"How can I help you?" Ana asked, challenging him. She made sure to remain a good distance from him, afraid that if she touched him she might not be able to resist him.

"Ana, what is going on with you and Alexander?" he asked, not hesitating in his question.

"I don't think that's an appropriate thing for you to ask," Ana replied, offended by the sudden inquisition, especially as she was the one who had seen him kiss another person.

"I'm just asking as someone who cares about you . . ." he started, but Ana put her hands up to stop him from talking.

"I'm sorry, but if there isn't anything else, I'd like to go and enjoy my break," Ana interrupted. Hunter sighed.

"Ana, I'm sorry. How many times do I have to say it? That woman kissed me." He tried to reason, but Ana didn't want to hear any more. This scene looked all too familiar to her past, and she was no longer interested in reliving her *past relationships*. If she was honest with herself, Alexander helped her realize she was worth more than her body could provide. She wanted to be with someone who saw that, and right now, Hunter was most definitely not that person.

"I know what I saw," Ana threw back at him, watching his expression change to . . . a look of *hurt*? *What game is he playing?* she thought to herself. *Do I want to play it?*

"And I know how I feel," Hunter insisted, catching Ana off guard.

"How you feel?" she asked as her tone softened. Hunter stood up and strode across his large office in a few steps. He stopped just in front of Ana

"Yes. I felt nothing for her," he whispered, his voice lowering.

"And for me?" Ana asked. Her heart pounded inside her chest, threatening to escape

"I'm still figuring it out . . . ." he said quietly, his voice seductive and smooth. He placed his hands around her waist, gripping tightly as he began kissing her. Ana let him pick up her body and carry her over to his sofa. Gently, he laid her down as he went back to tracing her body with his tongue, causing her toes to tingle with delight. Ana let out a quiet moan as Hunter pressed his body against hers. The mixture of exhilaration and the fear of getting caught filled her body. Hunter didn't seem to care as he removed his trousers and caressed her delicate figure. Ana kissed Hunter once again with a sense of longing to it. She didn't know what it was about him. He was so bad for her, and yet she knew she couldn't say no to him.

* * *

Ana looked at her watch. Harper was late. She tapped her heels on the marble floor.

"Hey, Ana!" Alexander waved at Ana as he made his way out of the elevator. "Where did you get to earlier?"

Ana blushed, remembering she had told Alexander she would meet him in the cafeteria. "Oh . . . oh my god, Alexander! I'm so sorry. Hunter asked me to help him with something and I completely lost track of time."

"No worries. I didn't wait that long," Alexander said, making it almost too obvious that he had, indeed, waited. "Hey look, I never know how to do this but . . . I was just wondering if you wanted to go and get a drink together?"

Alexander asked, shuffling his feet on the ground, afraid to look up at Ana.

Ana looked at Alexander, glad he wasn't meeting her eyes. He was asking her on a date? She liked him, but after what happened with Hunter, she wasn't sure she was emotionally available. At the same time, she didn't want to hurt him because, in another life, Alexander would have been the exact guy she would have loved to date. Steady, stable, funny.

"I can't tonight. I'm going out with Harper," she stammered, hoping that that was enough of an answer.

"What about another night? Any night you're free . . ." he asked, feeling a little braver. Now it was Ana's turn to shift uncomfortably. "Look . . . can I think about it?" Ana asked, causing Alexander to blush. They exchanged numbers, and to Ana's relief, Harper interrupted them by loudly telling the lobby that she needed the biggest drink possible. Alexander bid the ladies a good evening and made his way home as Harper and Ana, arm in arm, made their way to their favorite bar.

Sitting at the outdoor terrace, Ana closed her eyes to feel the breeze blow through her hair. Harper was busy drowning her sorrows in her large glass of wine while Ana sipped her martini. It had been a tiring week for them both, and the drinking therapy was much needed. Harper shared her office gossip for the week as Ana listened intently to the scandalous behavior of her colleagues.

"So where did you run off to this afternoon? I didn't see you for a while." Harper twirled the wine in her glass and wiggled her eyebrows.

Ana chuckled. It had been easy to lie to Alexander, but Harper knew her too well now.

"I was in Hunter's office," she said innocently.

"Uh-huh . . ." Harper clearly knew there was more to the story.

"We were, ya know . . . naked. On his couch."

"Anastasia Rose! Have you no shame?" The mock indignation made Ana laugh, but she also realized how challenging this un-relationship with Hunter was becoming. The hot and cold toward her all the time was making her head spin.

"It gets better. When you came into the lobby, Alexander was in the process of asking me out on a date."

Harper pouted. "I think you would make a cute couple!" she said, nodding with approval.

"I don't know. He's nice, but this thing with Hunter . . . He ignores me for weeks, kisses another woman. But then—"

"Sex in the office," Harper finished for her. "I don't know. I don't think 'humping Hunter' would care." Harper laughed, the drink taking over her normally prim and proper tone.

"What do you mean?" Ana asked, suddenly feeling anxious. She knew Hunter was smooth, but from the way Harper talked, it seemed like she knew much more.

Harper blushed. "I didn't mean anything by it. Really. Forget I said anything."

"Harper. Tell me. Please?"

"Look, Hunter has a certain . . . reputation around the office for wooing the ladies. Employees and clients. It's also rumored that he gets very unhappy if he doesn't get what he wants." Harper sighed. "Look, I'm only telling you this because Alexander's a nice guy. I'd hate for you to pass up a chance with a decent guy over that slime ball and get hurt in the process."

Ana felt her stomach tighten. Could she really have been that blind and stupid? Had she been missing the warning signals, excusing his closeness with other women in the office as him just being a good leader? As she thought about the ways other ladies in the office were always so quick to run to his office when summoned, she felt sick at the thought that she was not the first—or only—woman to have been seduced by him on his sofa.

"I didn't ruin your night, did I?" Harper asked, looking guilty. Ana shook her head and forced a smile on her face. Ordering another round of shots and drinks, Ana had a new mission: keep drinking until she forgot her romantic woes. She knew this wouldn't solve her problem, and she'd cut back on the drinking, but tonight seemed like an occasion that called for it.

Hours later, Ana and Harper were feeling good, leaning against each other for balance as they made their way to the exit. Just as they approached the doorway, Ana caught a glimpse of Hunter tucked away in a corner table with a slender brunette. They seemed to be enjoying each other's company as he leaned in and kissed her on the shoulder—exactly as he had with her. Despite the drinks she consumed, she was clearheaded enough to know it was he who leaned in. This time, there were no excuses. She was tired of being lied to and hurt. Taking her cell phone out of her bag, Ana texted Alexander: *I've thought about it. Drinks sound great!*

Chapter 10

The first date had been awkward. Ana and Alexander had done most of the "getting to know you" conversation at the office. It was clear to Ana that Alexander felt like she was out of his league. Something about him, though, made Ana feel calm. He was so unlike the other men she had dated. He was tender, soft, and passionate about the strangest things, but he treated her like she mattered. She'd been intoxicated by Hunter and his appreciation of her body, but Alexander saw more of her. That's why she agreed to the second and then a third date. She'd been writing in her journal about how excited she was to go to a bowling bar with him when her mom called.

"Hey, honey. Just wanted to check-in." Something in her mom's tone told her there was more of a reason than just checking in.

"Hey, Mom. Not much has changed from when I talked to you two days ago. Everything okay?"

"Yeah . . ." She heard a sigh. "I just missed you, I guess. Will you be okay tomorrow?"

Ana searched her brain to think about what "tomorrow" meant. She had her third date with Alexander but couldn't think of any other reason the day would be important. She looked at the date she'd written on her journal page and realized that "tomorrow" was the anniversary date of the day their whole world had come crashing down.

Ana sighed. "Mom, you don't have to do this every year. That's behind me. Us. I've moved on. It's just another day. Besides, I have a date with Alexander, and

I'm done punishing myself over something I had no control over. You should be done too."

"I know, Anastasia. It's just . . . sometimes I'm not sure you've really let go. You may not sit in your apartment and wallow, but the way you date these guys. You don't let them value you the way you deserve. I just worry about you." There was a long pause. "I just want you to be happy."

Ana didn't know what to say. She had an amazing relationship with her mom, who knew just as many details of her life as her journal did. But she rarely talked to her daughter like this.

"I'm going out with Alexander again if that makes you feel better. Third date."

"That's wonderful! Where are you going?"

Ana filled her mom in the details and asked how everything was back home. A text alerted a few minutes into family gossip and pulled Ana's attention away. It was from Hunter.

I need to see you. Please don't say no.

Ana cut the call short to her mom and thought about the best way to handle this. She and Alexander had been very careful about keeping their dating out of office gossip. Ana hadn't even told Harper yet. Could Hunter have found out? Or maybe he just wanted to lie to her again about the other women she'd consistently seen him with. Maybe he wanted to apologize and tell her he'd come to his senses and he was in love with her.

Whatever it was, she wanted to hear it. She sent him a reply that they could meet at a bar, but they'd have to make it quick because she had an appointment after. She didn't need to tell him that the appointment was her date with Alexander.

I'll be there. His reply came faster than she'd anticipated like he was waiting for hers.

Ana thought about what her mother had said. Why did she always chase after the guys that she knew weren't in it for the long haul. Was it them, or was it her that was afraid of commitment? Afraid of betrayal and getting her heart broken?

Alexander was the complete opposite of Hunter. She had to admit that her soft spot for him was growing. No matter what happened with Hunter, Alexander would be waiting for her when it was over. She just hoped it wouldn't be anything too drastic.

*　*　*

Ana walked into the bar and saw Hunter waiting for her. He was just as alluring and sexy as he'd always been. Ana knew she was going to have to work hard to make herself appear aloof. She cleared her throat and walked up next to him.

"Ana," he breathed. "You look stunning." He leaned toward her for a kiss, but she offered her cheek instead. She hadn't dressed for him tonight, but for Alexander. Her hair was down in soft waves. She wore a blouse with a pencil skirt that hugged her curves. It wasn't as outwardly sexy as something she would normally wear to go on a date.

Hunter picked up on her coolness. "Still mad at me?"

Ana looked down at the drink menu, avoiding him. "I'm just tired of being lied to, Hunter. I thought you had feelings for me, but it seems like you're interested in getting into everyone's pants. Not just mine."

"I said I was trying to figure it out." He brushed her hair behind her ear to see her face, but she wouldn't look at him. "I miss you. Say you'll come home with me tonight?" He'd leaned closer and was whispering in her ear again. His lips traced the soft curve of her earlobe, while one hand went around her waist and the other captured her wrist.

Her body's response was undeniable. She still wanted him, but she couldn't let herself get sucked into his games anymore.

"Hunter," she whispered, leaning away from him. "Please stop."

His grip on her wrist and her waist got stronger, almost painful. "I'm a patient man, Ana, but I don't take 'no' as an answer. That's what makes me so good at my job. Or haven't you figured that out by now?" The pressure on her wrist increased, but Ana managed to pull away from him.

She backed up, almost running into the person next to her. She half-smiled at Hunter, trying not to let the tears she felt overrun her lashes. "If you'll just excuse me a minute? I need to powder my nose."

Ana walked quickly to the bathroom and splashed cold water on her face as soon as the door closed. She looked at herself in the mirror, then pulled up her sleeve to see the red fingerprints Hunter had left on her wrist. How was she going to get out of this? There was no way for her to leave without Hunter stopping her. Maybe she could signal the bartender for help somehow, or make enough of a scene that Hunter would leave her alone. Her heart skipped a beat at her next thought. *What if Hunter tried to get her fired?* She tried to quickly move past that thought. She was known for being great at what she did. In her short time at Startling, she'd already gained much success. Something in her stomach told her she needed to be careful navigating this situation. This was unchartered territory for her. She didn't want to lose her job.

Pushing her thoughts away, she collected herself, dabbed at her wet face with a paper towel, and knew that no matter what, she had to face this head-on. She'd done it before, and she knew she was brave enough to do it again.

She pulled the door open to meet her fate and almost collided with Alexander.

"Ana!" He caught her before she could topple. "Ana! Are you here with Hunter?" Alexander seemed confused and maybe a little panicked.

"No, I . . . He said he wanted to talk about work stuff." Ana wasn't sure he'd believe her, but she had to try. "Wait. Are you spying on me?"

He looked like she'd hit him. "No! I got here early and grabbed us a table; from there, I could see you two at the bar." Alexander got quiet and ducked his head. "It didn't look like he wanted to talk about work. I saw what happened, and I saw you run away. I also saw him slip something into your drink once you left for the bathroom. I understand if you'd want him over me, but I couldn't let you go back there without telling you."

Ana couldn't believe what she was hearing. The blood drained from her face. Hunter was obviously determined and prepared to have her back—by any means necessary. Alexander softly held her hands and turned them over to see the red marks. Ana's cheeks flushed in embarrassment. He looked up at Ana with what looked like anger and sympathy and she was momentarily concerned about what he would do.

"I don't choose him over you," Ana said softly. "But I don't know how to get out of here without him seeing me. Or us. Did he see you?"

"I don't think so. He doesn't notice anyone who isn't female at the office, so I doubt he would notice me here." Alexander looked around and grabbed her hand. "Come on. I bet we can slip through the kitchen."

Ana followed along behind him as he pulled her through the busy kitchen and out of a back door.

He looked at her seriously when they got outside. "That's not exactly how I thought our third date was going to go."

Ana giggled trying to make light of the situation. "Me either." She looked down at their clasped hands then back up at him. "Thank you. For saving me. You're a real knight in shining armor."

Alexander blushed. "Want to grab some Chinese?" He pointed down the road.

"Love to."

* * *

By their fifth date, Alexander had finally managed to convince Ana to come back to his house so that he could cook her what he promised to be his world-famous spaghetti Bolognese. Alexander sang along to the radio as he stirred. Ana sat on a chair watching him as she sipped on a glass of red wine, trying to forget about what had happened with Hunter. He hadn't been in the office for a while and could only assume he was traveling again. She noticed Alexander's high notes and laughed as he shook his hips to the music. Getting up, Ana danced alongside him. Wearing a baggy shirt with rolled-up jeans, Ana for once let herself loose. With Alexander, she couldn't help but just be herself: no heels, no fancy outfit. With him, she could enjoy herself and not be afraid of embarrassing herself in front of him. *Mainly because he was more likely to do something embarrassing first*, she thought, laughing to herself.

During dinner, Alexander entertained Ana with his impersonations of their colleagues. He gave them exaggerated personalities encouraged by Ana's hysterical laughter. She found herself clinging to the table for support. Alexander stopped for a moment, wiping a stray bit of sauce from Ana's lip. Ana blushed, feeling butterflies in her stomach from his touch. Ana leaned in and closed her eyes. Alexander's lips brushed hers gently and slowly. She looked at Alexander. His eyes were closed too. Ana kissed him again, pulling away quickly before she got too carried away.

"Ana..." he spoke slowly. Ana looked at him to show she was listening. "I want to tell you something..." He struggled with his words, the nerves wavering in his voice. Alexander fidgeted, seeming to regret having started this conversation already. "I know this is so soon, but I really like you..." Ana smiled. She could tell from the look on his face that he was anxious.

"I like you too, Alexander. A lot!" she said reassuringly, and she realized as she said it that she actually meant it, too.

"It's just... I can tell I'm falling for you already, but I can't fall for you until I tell you this."

Ana felt the anxiety pass on to her. She prepared herself to listen but was afraid of what he was going to admit. She had been on cloud nine for the past few weeks after he'd saved her and as their blossoming romance grew.

Alexander took a deep breath. "Ana, I don't talk about my parents. I don't know if you noticed." He finally looked at Ana, but she remained silent. "My parents died when I was a teenager. I don't think I really cried at their funeral. They were alcoholics and had gotten in an accident. Drunk driving," he said. His sentences flowed into one another in his eagerness to get it all out. Ana reached across the table as she put her hand reassuringly on his.

"I'm sorry, Alexander. I can't imagine what that's like," she said, trying to comfort him.

"That's not it. You see, I don't think I cried because part of me was relieved they were gone." Alexander's face reddened as he felt his guilt overwhelm him. "I've never told anyone this, but they used to beat me. Whenever they'd drink, they'd both go into this rage and use me as a punching bag. I grew to hate them."

Ana didn't know how to respond. She watched as Alexander transformed from the curly-haired, handsome man she had grown to know to a small, meek kid afraid of his own shadow—much like her old self. Still, she held his trembling hand.

"When the police came to pick me up from school, I knew what was coming. It's like I'd spent my whole childhood waiting for the news to come about them being drunk and reckless. I remember being relieved they didn't hurt anyone else. It didn't hit me that I was all alone and without a family for years. I'd always felt alone for as long as I could remember anyway." Alexander took another deep breath and so did Ana. She had not realized it, but she had been holding her breath since he started sharing his story. Alexander's eyes glinted with unshed tears as Ana squeezed his hand tighter.

"Thank you for trusting me enough to share that with me. I'm sorry that happened, but you do realize how amazing you are, right?" Ana briefly wondered if this should be her opportunity to share her past, but she didn't feel ready. Something inside of her told her she needed to keep it to herself, so she did. She stayed quiet about her past in order to help Alexander with his.

"It doesn't change the way I feel about you," Ana told Alexander as they stood up to embrace. Alexander swayed Ana in his arms, dancing to the slow music on the radio. He started singing to her. He had a beautifully melodic voice, and Ana closed her eyes as she marveled at the romance of that moment. Once again, they found themselves face to face. Alexander leaned in to kiss her, the tenderness between them turning into hunger. Ana pulled Alexander closer to her so that there wasn't any distance between them. They made their way to the bedroom, kissing and touching each other's exposed skin.

As they reached the edge of the bed, Ana pulled away. Panting, Alexander looked at her confused.

"I'm sorry," Ana said apologetically. Her body begged her to carry on. Her heart pounded loudly, her mind telling her to calm down. "I'm sorry, Alexander. I want to take this slow . . ." she explained, looking at him. To her surprise, he told her he understood. "It's just so typical of me to rush into things. I want this to be different. I want us to take this slow."

Alexander nodded. "I can't say I'm not disappointed, but I care about you and respect you too much to ever pressure you into something you're not ready for." He eased the tension with another impersonation, causing Ana to fall into fits of giggles again. She kissed him to thank him for his decency. They spent the rest of the date lying in bed in each other's arms watching TV.

Chapter 11

Alexander opened the door to their suite. Ana gasped as she took in the room. A giant glass wall served as the window, overlooking the bright lights of Vegas. Ana squealed with excitement as she pushed Alexander into the emperor bed and jumped on after him. Laying in luxurious comfort, Ana turned to Alexander and kissed him.

"Can you believe this place?" She gasped, catching her breath from all the excitement. Alexander took a look around the room. Every inch of it looked so expensive he was afraid to touch anything.

"Wow, the perks of being a teacher's pet," joked Alexander as he kissed Ana on the forehead.

"Hey, this was well earned! Perks of being so amazing at my job!" She giggled, as she took in her surroundings. This was one of the best benefits to her job, winning big clients meant she would get free trips to fabulous places, and now she had someone to enjoy it with.

Ana had been pushing herself to exceed expectations, especially since her encounter with Hunter had made her conscious that he would retaliate in some way when she disappeared. So far, he had been quiet, barely acknowledging her when they were in the same meetings. It had unnerved her at first, but then she grew to not care as it made her job a lot easier. No more feeling jealous whenever he spoke to another woman, no more worrying about what he thought or how she dressed, and no more feeling like she was not enough. She had worked hard to grow from who she used to be. Plus, there was Alexander, who loved every part of her even though he knew what she looked like in the mornings and what her temper could be like before coffee. That is how she knew she was serious about him.

Alexander stared out of the window, waiting for Ana to finish putting on her makeup before they went out. He looked in awe at the phenomenal view and how small the cars looked below him. He was nervous. He was not sure if Ana noticed, but he hoped his palms would stop sweating by the time she was ready to go.

Ana spritzed her favorite Marc Jacobs perfume, looking at herself in the mirror. Her hair shone its usual radiant golden blonde. She was dressed in one of her favorite party dresses. It was flirty but still classy. And while her towering heels hurt her feet, they made her legs look fantastic. Yes, she looked good but felt even better. She was excited to see where Alexander was taking her for dinner. Looking at her boyfriend, she watched as he stared thoughtfully out at the view. Ana walked slowly over to where Alexander stood. She liked how he had dressed up for their date. Looking so handsome, Ana couldn't help but admire their reflection in the glass. Ana hugged Alexander from behind, breathing in his cologne. Alexander turned to hug Ana back. Kissing her on the forehead, he cherished the moment of peace they had together.

Ana reflected once more on how different Alexander was from Hunter. In his arms, she felt cherished and loved. Hunter had made her feel like an object—from the way he spoke to her to the way he fucked her. He was rough and demanding in every sense. Alexander had opened up another side of her with his tenderness. When they had finally made love, he'd taken his time. They'd explored together, and Ana felt like new worlds had opened to her under his hands and body. Could sex be called healing? Because if it could, she thought that was exactly what Alexander had done for her.

At dinner, Ana and Alexander sat at their table, gazing out the window. If they thought the view from their hotel room was beautiful, then the sights from The Top of The World restaurant were simply breathtaking. Ana couldn't believe what she was seeing. Las Vegas was so far the best work trip she had been on, and it was even better that she could share this first experience with Alexander. Their evening was spent drinking wine, staring out at the view, and playing games of eye spy. There was something about Alexander's view on life that made Ana live a childhood that she had never experienced. He brought out her fun and goofy side, something she had tried to get rid of once she started taking life a little more seriously. Alexander taught her how she could be both a serious successful businesswoman and a silly, happy-go-lucky Ana.

Alexander fidgeted, signaling to Ana he had something he wanted to talk about. She was used to this tick of his now, so she placed a comforting hand on top of his.

"Are you okay?" she asked. Alexander looked up at Ana. He had been rehearsing this in his head for so long in front of the mirror that he had memorized what he wanted to say.

"Ana, I love you . . ." he blurted out, completely forgetting the romantic spiel he had practiced. Ana started laughing from the sudden outburst, quickly catching herself.

"I love you too," she said, kissing Alexander's shocked face.

"But you laughed . . ." he stammered, reddening with embarrassment.

"Yes, because I thought you were going to propose," she admitted, feeling a little embarrassed herself. Alexander laughed with her.

"I'm not that impulsive!" he responded. Ana took a breath and looked out the window, without really thinking about it she waved her hand.

"I am."

Alexander gazed at her, realizing what she had said. Ana blushed. "I mean . . . I'm not saying I would have said yes. I'm just saying . . ."

"That you would say yes if I asked?" Alexander finished for her, enjoying the sight of Ana squirming with discomfort. He burst out laughing again which helped relax Ana. "So if I asked and you said yes, we'd basically be engaged?" Alexander asked, continuing their joke.

"Yes, but I don't really like the idea of long engagements." Ana finally joined in on the joke. "So when would you want the wedding to be?"

"Now seem like a good time?" Ana shrugged, watching Alexander to see his reaction. His face straightened as he searched on Ana's face for any sign of a smirk that would give her true intentions away.

"Are you being serious?" he asked, trying hard not to feel excited in case she told him she was joking, but Ana kept her face straight as she nodded.

"We're in Vegas. We could get married anytime during this trip!" She smiled, looking back at the breathtaking view.

"Then maybe I was going to propose . . ." Alexander said, following her gaze at the lights below.

"Then maybe I would say yes," she replied, taking his hand once again.

"Are we really doing this?" Alexander asked again, still unsure of how he should be feeling. Maybe it was his fault that they were always trying to play jokes and make each other laugh, but his heart pounded loudly under his shirt. He had just told Ana he loved her, the first woman he did that with in many years. He had shared so much of himself already, and whenever he looked at her, all he could think of was spending every day making her laugh and feel loved.

    Ana finally looked back at him. When she was with him, she felt safe, secure. The nightmares that would make visits to her at least once a month had barely made an appearance since Alexander entered her life. Her self-confidence had grown as he showed her how a woman should be treated, and most importantly, he loved her family. Her relationship with her mom and Avery always remained a constant throughout her life, sometimes so much so that she felt she would never be where she was if it had not been for them. He had taught her she was truly capable of loving, something she had been afraid was impossible. Sure, it was sudden and not planned. But why not? If she was already thinking about spending every day with him, why not start today? Ana flashed him her biggest smile "When in Vegas!"

* * *

    Their ceremony had taken less than ten minutes, at a little chapel off the Strip. Ana didn't know why, but she was nervous about their wedding night as Alexander fiddled with the key to the hotel room. After he got the door open, he lifted her off of her feet and carried her across the threshold.

    "Alexander!" She giggled as she adjusted herself so they could both fit through the door.

    "I want to at least do this part right." He sounded happy but serious and the laughter died in Ana's throat.

    He laid her gently on the bed. The lights of Las Vegas gleamed through the curtains. Alexander knelt at her feet and kissed the top of each one. He removed her shoes and stockings and caressed the backs of her thighs.

"Just a sec…" He got up and found his phone. Soft music soon came from the small speaker and he set it down on the nightstand next to Ana.

"I thought maybe we could take bath together…If you want."

This was something Ana had never seen first-hand. She'd heard that romance like this existed, but having it in front of her made her suddenly unsure of what she should do next. She could handle fucking, but intimacy?

She smiled reassuringly. "I'd like that."

So this is what true love feels like, she thought to herself.

Alexander moved over to her and reached his hand out so she could stand. He turned her around and unzipped her dress, placing kisses on each shoulder as the fabric fell from them. She shuddered. He helped her step out of her dress and led her into the bathroom. He lifted her on top of the vanity and wrapped a warm towel around her while she waited. The tap squeaked loudly when he turned it, and they laughed, but it didn't change the mood. Ana hadn't felt this kind of anticipation in a long time.

Alexander undressed himself while Ana watched. He had a certain beauty to the structure of his body, the way his hips dipped into the planes of his stomach, the small patch of hair on his chest. He stood naked before her and she felt completely pulled to him. He was her husband now. That meant something more than just being a word casually tossed around. She felt the weight of the meaning behind it.

She reached up and caressed his chest. He moaned a little and leaned into her. His arms reached behind her to unhook her bra and help her out of her delicate panties. He paused at her thighs and placed gentle kisses on each, up her stomach, one on each breast, and finally stopped at her lips.

Ana buzzed. His body was so warm and firm against hers. She felt safe. She felt cared for. His tenderness was so unlike anything she'd ever experienced and it made her dizzy. Alexander trailed his fingers up and down her spine while his lips and tongue explored her mouth. His hand stilled at the base of her neck, while the other found her hip.

So this is what I've been missing, Ana thought.

The water sounded like it was reaching the right level, and he pulled away to turn the tap off. Her fingertips danced across his arms, his chest, his back. His eyes looked into hers and she felt only love radiating from them.

"The water's gonna get cold if we stand here much longer," he kissed her smiling mouth and pressed more firmly against her. "Care to join me, wife?" He helped her off the vanity.

Ana nodded. Words didn't seem important. She wanted to savor every moment of her wedding night with this man. She felt her heart and body flutter and thought that, at last, she might finally know what true love meant.

CHAPTER 12

Ana walked into the office on Monday morning, glowing from the magical trip she had been on with Alexander. Harper waved at her from her desk and signaled they needed to catch up. Ana's phone rang at her desk. Giving Harper the five-minute signal, Ana picked up her phone.

"Hello, Ana speaking," she said in her telephone voice.

"Hi Ana, it's Zack. Can you come into my office?" Ana's stomach tightened. He had a weird tone to his voice that made Ana nervous. This was it. She was in trouble. She racked her brain for everything bad she had done since she started working at Starling Enterprise. Sure, she had come in late a few times. Though it was usually after a work event where she had been encouraged by a senior member of the board to drink a little too much. Or was it the Vegas itinerary she had printed out using company stationery? Or worse, had her non-relationship with Hunter finally been exposed. Since Ana had started making a name for herself as a top employee, she had held her breath waiting for her fairy tale life to suddenly come shattering down around her.

Ana bit her lip as she slowly made her way to Zack's office. Clara passed her walking in the opposite direction and winking. What did that mean? Ana started feeling faint. She had been with the company for over a year now and had worked incredibly hard. She had been bringing big money in too, enough to earn her position. Ana knocked on the door and was greeted by Zack, asking her to come in. Ana walked into the office, nervously straightening her skirt. Surprised, she saw Zack at his desk with Hunter by his side as well as a few other directors she had briefly met at meetings, each holding a glass of champagne. Zack handed one to Ana as she looked at them all confused.

"Thank you for joining us, Ana." Zack guided her toward the middle of the room. "I asked you in here because I wanted to talk to you about something, or rather, we'd like to talk to you about something."

Feeling sick, Ana looked frantically at Hunter who gave away no sign of what this conversation was going to be about. For a brief moment, Ana allowed her mind to go wild with worry. Surely Zack would not embarrass her in front of a group of people, would he? She questioned herself, feeling like he was taking way too long to explain why she had been called.

"We've been so impressed with your performance since you started here. You've really led your department to a level of success that we didn't anticipate in a new team." Ana breathed a sigh of relief to herself as Hunter gave a reassuring nod. Finally, he was showing some kind of emotion, a slight smile, but she knew for him that meant he was in a good mood.

"Having said that, we've thought long and hard on what we're about to share with you. Greg will be retiring from his role as director of client relations, and through some very positive recommendations, we'd like to offer you the opportunity to take over his role."

Greg, probably one of the oldest men in the room, nodded to Ana with a smile, raising his glass at her.

"We'll go over the finer details shortly, but since we already had your future team members in my office—should you accept the offer, of course—we thought it might be nice to celebrate your promotion all together!" Zack beamed at Ana, waiting for her to respond.

Speechless, Ana knew she would have to say something. She thought quickly about what she could say without making her sound like a complete idiot.

"Thank you, Zack . . . everyone." She looked around the room at the smiling faces. Even Hunter couldn't resist sneaking a wink in. "I'm so honored. I . . . I am just so excited to be able to continue on with what I already know has been fantastic work led by Greg." Ana nodded to Greg. Again, he raised his glass. This time, everyone else followed suit, and they clinked their glasses and, in unison, took a sip.

I guess this is what it's like to be part of The Boy's Club, Ana thought happily to herself. *Drinking champagne at 9 a.m. on a Monday morning.*

There was a knock at the door as Zack called for the person on the other side to enter. Clara came in as she told her boss he had a visitor waiting for him in the lobby. Zack thanked her, but before Clara walked back out of the office, she spotted the champagne.

"Oh, Ana. Congratulations!" Ana thanked her and expressed her gratitude for the promotion. Looking doubly excited, Clara squealed with happiness.

"This really is your month! Two amazing things in one!" Zack laughed at Clara's youthful personality; he enjoyed her happiness for just being happy.

"Two, Ana?" Zack asked, causing Ana to blush. Deep inside her, she hoped Clara would not say what Ana thought she knew.

"Didn't she tell you? Ana and Alexander got married this weekend!" Clara blurted out excitedly. "Congratulations again, Ana!" And with that, Clara left the office.

Zack stood speechless for a moment. "I had no idea you and Alexander were dating, Ana. Nevertheless, what exciting news for you both! Congratulations!" Again, the gentlemen raised their glasses to celebrate her. Ana's blush deepened. She glanced over at Hunter, whose smile instantly vanished.

The men said their goodbyes as Hunter made a hasty exit out of Zack's office. He took long strides down the corridor and into the elevator. He pressed for the top floor, walking into the lobby he made his way toward the receptionist. "Jane, I'd like to speak to Richard."

"Mr. Harvey is going into a meeting soon, Hunter. Can it wait?" she asked, scrolling through her boss's calendar on the computer. "It's urgent, Jane. I need to see him now. The CEO of this company must receive this information."

Hunter leaned onto the table, eager to get her to comply. He had a few seconds to decide whether he was going to go ahead and do this. Since the night that Ana had rejected him, he had thought of all the ways he could ensure she paid for the embarrassment she had caused him. She would find that bruising Hunter's ego was much more dangerous than she could ever imagine. If it were not for him, Ana would not be getting this promotion, something he had recommended her for as he had thought she was compliant with his requests. He never dreamed he would be turned down for some unknown, unimportant analyst who had very little power compared to him. Hunter felt his anger building. He gave Ana what she had in this company, and it was time that she learned he could also take it all away.

Chapter 13

It had been two weeks since Hunter went into Robert's office to share that Ana had married someone on her team. Robert hadn't taken any action yet and Hunter was tired of waiting. It was rare for him to work out in the office gym, but he had been traveling so much lately that he felt the need to work out and didn't have enough time to go out before his meeting. He flexed his muscles in the mirror, admiring how little effort he needed to make to get himself so toned. He made his way to the treadmill and started off with a brisk jog.

After warming up, he began his sprint, sweat starting to bead on his forehead. He kept his pace, determined to beat his personal best on his five-mile run. Hunter was strong because he would always tell himself to stay hungry, focused, and determined. That is probably what made him so good at his job—so good at everything. Yes, for men like Hunter, most things came easy because he knew just what he wanted and was never ashamed of it. No one ever said no to him. He could be persuasive like that. Some even called him charming.

It was not until he met Ana that he had experienced being defied by a woman. He had given her so much: the job she was in and recommending her for her promotion. And how did she repay him? By leaving him for a loser like Alexander. He was not even aware of who Alexander was until the office gossip circled about how quiet Alexander had won the heart of the office eye candy. If anything, Hunter felt that her behavior was inappropriate.

With his anger mounting, his speed quickened. He did not feel guilty for bringing her unprofessional behavior to their CEO. He was not going to let her continue her life without being punished for the disrespect she had shown him. He felt no qualms about being angered by her rejection. She clearly didn't know him. She did not realize the kindness he was showing her by giving her his time. He clenched his fist and ran faster, using his frustration at Ana as motivation to push harder in his workout. When he met her, she was nothing—nothing compared to him. She owed him her career at Starling. She owed him for the life she was living, and soon, she would know about it.

Hunter finished his run, happy he had beaten his personal best. He smirked, finding it funny how anger pushes you to perform better. He made his way to the weights just as a few other colleagues joined him to work out. Hunter smiled politely and focused on working his muscles hard. A guy he recognized from the third floor was talking about a woman with killer legs. It caught Hunter's attention as he inserted himself into the conversation, enjoying the male bravado his colleagues were showing.

"Ana's by far the hottest piece of ass in the boardroom" another guy piped up. Hunter's smile fell as he realized the very person who caused him anger was the topic of conversation. Finally, he had an easy opening to tell them what he really thought of her.

"I heard she was easy," Hunter began as he started to sow seeds of doubt over her integrity. "Easy to sleep with, easy to influence. It makes you question what kinds of tricks she uses to secure clients, huh?" Hunter laughed. The guys around him laughed uneasily. They looked uncomfortable, but in a large office such as theirs, he had no doubt this new gossip about Ana would spread like wildfire.

"I guess I did wonder how she was dominating the markets right now, especially since it's been so tough for so many others," one colleague began.

"And I did think it was strange how quickly she and Alexander got married. Makes you wonder what she's trying to cover," said another.

Hunter smirked again. Saying his goodbyes, he turned on his heel and decided his work was done for the day.

* * *

Ana walked into the office feeling ready to dominate yet another working week. Her heels made a rhythmic noise on the marble floors accompanying her happy mood. Ana wished Jennifer the receptionist a good morning and got into the elevator.

Inside were a few fellow colleagues getting their day started with cups of coffee. The usually chatty buzz fell into silence as she walked in. *Strange*, Ana thought. She did not allow paranoid thoughts to take over. She could feel eyes on her as she made her way out of the elevator and walked to her office. Shutting the door behind her, Ana breathed a sigh of relief. She had felt the tension of the elevator and was wondering what it was about the sudden change in mood that caused her stomach to hurt. She quite often had these gut instincts and could sense when trouble was coming. Trying to shake her mind from it, Ana made her way to the coffee station.

Ana was greeted by another fellow senior manager offering him a coffee too.

"How was your weekend, Greg?" she asked. Her colleague talked about his rock climbing adventures, casually flexing his muscles from under his suit. Was it just Ana, or was he behaving a little differently? Ana talked about her spa retreat, twisting her neck and giving it a little massage.

"It did wonders for my body!" she said, remembering how much stress she felt her break took off of her. Greg raised his eyebrows.

"You're still looking a little tense now, Anastasia," he said, stepping forward.

Ana laughed.

"Maybe you need another massage?" he asked, his voice getting lower. He reached over to Ana and pulled her toward him, just a little too close for Ana's comfort.

"No, I'm fine," Ana replied, feeling the sudden change in atmosphere disconcerting, but Greg was not listening. He looked her up and down, admiring the way her suit clung to her toned body. He licked his lips, placing his hand forcefully on Ana's shoulders, and pulled her in closer as she tried to move away.

Ana was not new to sexual harassment, but she still found herself unprepared to respond to Greg. Her hands were trembling, and she felt like that little girl in the garage all those years ago. In the middle of Ana's mind racing through all those memories, Clara walked in. Greg stopped in his tracks as wide-eyed Clara apologized. Ana realized what a compromising position Clara had caught them in and how she must be interpreting the situation.

Ana rushed to try to explain. "Wait, Clara. It is not what you think." Ana found herself going red trying to explain, but Clara backed out equally red, running down the corridor like she was afraid. Ana turned to face Greg, straightening her back she let out an angry, silent scream.

"What the hell are you doing?" she whispered quietly to him, trying not to yell at him in anger. Greg laughed, brushing aside the rejection.

"I was just kidding, Ana. Don't get your panties in a twist." And with that, he grabbed the coffee Ana had made him and walked out. Completely shocked at what had happened, Ana stared at the space he had just left.

When will this injustice ever end? she thought to herself. And then it dawned on her. *Maybe I have to play like a man but win like a woman.* She wasn't sure what made her think of this. Maybe it was the years of sexual assault, her many conversations with Grace, years of feeling less than worthy—all the pain she had experienced. Who knew? But Ana was growing tired of dealing with this bullshit.

Ana tucked herself away in her office, making it explicitly clear to Harper that she was not to be disturbed until her board meeting. For a few hours, she had peace as she did her paperwork, working out how she could improve this financial quarter for her team. Ana loved the exhilaration she got from being able to work out complicated matters and how strong and smart it made her feel to be so accomplished on a Monday morning. Finally, she had something positive she could present at the meeting. Sweeping her paperwork into her hands, she made her way to the boardroom.

She walked through the busy main office, eyes following her, with a bright smile. She wished everyone she met along the way a happy morning. If Ana had eyes on the back of her head, she would have seen the chaos descending around her at her expense. As she walked with pride, her colleagues smiled at her but gossiped behind her back about what Clara had witnessed that morning. The not-so-innocent gossip Hunter had started was making its way to the various teams the other colleagues at the gym worked in. Just as he masterminded, his plan was falling into place.

In the boardroom, Ana presented her changes to a somewhat uninterested group of people. She could sense their mind was elsewhere and had even caught a few of the men whispering amongst each other. Ana felt herself feeling hot with frustration. She had woken up in such a good mood, and over the course of the day, she felt like there was a change in the air. She was fairly sure she knew what or who was behind it—Hunter. All she kept telling herself was, *"Play like a man and win like a woman."*

Ana shrugged off her suit jacket. One guy wolf-whistled, causing the rest of the men in the room to laugh.

Ana felt the color drain from her face. She sauntered up to Ian, the one who wolf-whistled, and got right up in his face so only a few could hear, whispering, "Say something like that again and I'll walk straight from here to Mr. Haskell's office and have you fired!" She turned on her heel and headed back to the front to continue her presentation. Ian called out, "You wouldn't dare."

Ana stopped dead in her tracks, spun around so fast her hair whipped at her face, and said, "I am the one who just got promoted, and you've been here how long, Ian? Five years?" Everyone in the room looked at Ian, who was looking down at the table. "Ian, try that again and see if am bluffing; I have his ear. Do you?" Ana said loudly so the entire room heard her. She didn't know where this sudden confidence was coming from, but she had enough of men abusing her and overexerting their power over her. It was time for her to take a stance. Once back at the front of the room, she completed her presentation with no more interruptions. After the meeting, she walked directly back to her office and closed the door. She couldn't believe her boldness, but she was proud of herself.

Whether by coincidence or not, most of the senior leaders in Starling were men. She was often the envy of the other women in the office. Many had worked years and hadn't gotten as far as Ana did. She often had to remind herself that she worked incredibly hard to get to her position and more than earned her keep for the company, managing a portfolio of multimillion-dollar clients. A knock on the door startled her back to reality.

Ana . . ." Westley came in looking sheepish. "Mr. Haskell asked to see you in his office." Ana felt the blood drain from her face. Zack had been busy—very busy. He was in the middle of some very big company changes, and she knew that if he was taking the time to see her, it meant something serious was happening. *Perhaps he heard about what happened in the meeting?* Ana straightened her suit and went to her boss's office.

"Hi, Ana. Please take a seat," Zack said in a strangely formal manner. Ana felt the knot in her stomach tighten. *What was happening?* she thought to herself.

"Zack . . . is something wrong?" Ana asked, feeling her nerves get the best of her. Zack sighed and stayed silent for a moment. The silence told her enough. She was in trouble. She didn't think she had anything to feel guilty about. Anything she'd done had been well within company policy. She went above and beyond for everyone in this office. Surely she'd be able to convince Zack of that.

Finally, Zack spoke, shifting uncomfortably in his seat, his usual calm demeanor, but he was more uptight and stiff than usual. "Ana, we need to talk about your behavior and the way you conduct yourself in the office."

Ana's mouth dropped. "Zack, please let me explain about the meeting today. It was—" Ana began, but Zack held his hand up at her.

"It has been brought to our attention that you've been conducting some inappropriate behavior with some colleagues and those junior to you," he started again.

"You're kidding, right?" Ana laughed, scanning his face for any sign of a prank.

"No, Ana. It has been reported to us that you've been having inappropriate relations with various members of our team, and quite freely, at corporate functions as well as in the office itself."

"Did this come from Clara? She thinks she knows what she saw this morning, but I can explain."

Again, Zack raised his hand up at Ana to stop her from talking. "Please stop, Anastasia. This is already incredibly difficult," he said as he put down his hand and rested it on his desk. Ana could tell Zack was really struggling with what he was about to say. Ana was nervous about what was going to come next. She tried to steady her hands by sitting on them.

"While we cannot disclose where our information came from, I can tell you, Ana, that if you keep your ear close to the ground, you will know that we've had multiple sources." Zack picked up some documents from his desk. "We've had a worrisome complaint about inappropriate behavior during a work trip, wherein it was said that you and two other colleagues engaged in a threesome. Ana, it is not our business what you do in your own time, but when on a business trip, you are representing the company."

The anger in Ana rose to new heights as she tried to take in some cooling breaths. She had no idea what he was talking about. "I need you to understand that Harper, while your friend is still your junior and–

"Harper?" Ana shouted a little too loudly. "You think I had a threesome with Harper and someone else? Why? I'm guessing this is the work trip where Harper, James, and I, after a quiet, relaxing meal, decided to end our night enjoying the hotel amenities of the hot tub before retiring to our *own* rooms while all the others went out partying?"

"Let me see if I'm following you. A group of senior men go out partying and are seen with women that are either their assistant or their junior. Two others and I have a quiet evening in with no drinking or partying, and yet . . . I'm in trouble? Someone fabricated this ridiculous story and you bought it, Mr. Haskell? I'm now a married woman, remember? Oh right, to most men in this office that doesn't seem to matter. What about you; does it matter to you?" Ana retorted a little more firmly than she meant to. Zack remained quiet so Ana kept on.

"Zack, I never go to the parties because you and I know what goes on at them, so I purposely stay away!" Ana didn't know if she was angry or sad. What she did know—with complete certainty—was that she was not going down without a fight—not this time. Especially after what had happened in her morning meeting and having to put Ian and the others in their place. She knew Harper would not have said anything, so clearly, her colleague James, who had offered the threesome as a joke and was outright rejected had said something.

"You get that this all sounds absolutely ridiculous, right? I'm happily married, Zack. We are still newlyweds for goodness' sake. This is not fair, actually; it is sexual harassment and slander, and both are illegal. You and I are both well aware of what goes on between employees behind closed doors at corporate functions. In fact, at our last event in San Diego, one of the new young salesmen, Peter I think his name was, showed up the next day sporting a black eye! Do you know how he got that, Zack? Did you ever look into that event?"

"No, I didn't, Ana. I never heard about this before." Ana kept up with her questioning, trying to make her point about how unfair it was, how unjust this all was; this was her reputation at stake.

With her anger rising, she continued, "He got that because he went to a new associate's hotel room, banging on her door in the middle of the night, and she protected herself. No one knows what she needed to protect herself from because she didn't dare file a complaint as a new associate; she had to protect herself, Zack. Is that the kind of company you want? A company where women are sexually harassed and too scared to say anything in fear of retaliation? Much like you're doing to me right now! But guess what? Nothing happened to Peter. In fact, I saw a memo about a promotion he recently received. But here I am in trouble, even though I'm innocent and have been avoiding parties for this exact reason. But you are still taking the good ol' 'boys' side and bringing up baseless allegations against me!" Ana was almost shouting at this time.

"Ana, please calm down; I didn't hear about Peter until now."

"Of course you haven't. That's the whole point," Ana retorted in disgust. She was so disappointed in Zack. He had been her mentor in many ways, and she was beyond disgusted. She was disappointed. She felt betrayed by someone she trusted.

"Yes, I do agree this doesn't sound like you. I'll look into the other allegations, but this is not about him right now. This is about you. There have been multiple reports of inappropriate sexual behavior within the workplace, such as having sex in a bathroom with a colleague; we're also conducting an investigation into how your relationship with Alexander started."

Ana raged her temples pulsing from a headache starting to form.

"Your position in the company has brought questions on the propriety of forming a relationship with a coworker who is a junior to you."

"When Alexander and I started dating, I was not his senior. When we notified HR of our relationship, we had requested he be removed from my team to take away any risk of untoward behavior or thoughts. We followed protocol. You know that because I told you, or do you not remember?" Ana said quietly, trying her hardest to refrain from letting sarcasm into her tone.

"Ana, there's a lot of mounting questions that are not being answered."

"That's the first *true* statement you've said throughout this whole meeting," Ana retorted.

Ana was starting to get tired of this game. "Do you believe any of them, Mr. Haskell?" Ana asked, taking a seat, and looking at her boss directly in his eye—the boss she had been working so hard for, the boss she had grown to become friends with, the boss she had been an open book with.

"The board feels it would be best for you to allow us to complete our investigations."

"Please answer my question, Zack. Do you believe any of them?"

"Ana, it's not about whether or not I believe—"

This time, Ana raised her hand up at Zack.

"That's all I need to know. You're right, Mr. Haskell. What I do in my personal time is none of your business. By all means, do whatever investigation you need to do, but please know that any impropriety that was and is done will be noted and reported right back."

"Ana, please do not make this difficult."

Ana got up and started to walk out. "Is there anything else? I worked hard here, and everyone knows it, including you. I will not go down without a fight. This is my reputation!"

"Ana." Zack sighed, his discomfort throughout the conversation had increased. Ana felt a slight pang of guilt. She knew he was not the one pulling strings. Part of her thought Hunter was involved in some way. It had to be him. How many colleagues had she had sex with in a bathroom? One. That one was Hunter. Walking out of Zack's office, Ana made her way to Hunter's office.

His assistant, Tristan, smiled at Ana. Clearly, he had not been one of the office gossips as he was one of the few smiling happily at her like nothing was wrong like she was not the office slut.

"Hi, Ana!" he called. "Can I help you?"

"Tristan, I need to speak to Hunter," she said a little too forcefully.

"Sorry, no can do. He has asked not to be disturbed today," Tristan responded apologetically.

"Is he in a meeting right now?" Ana asked. Tristan shook his head. Ana walked past him and opened Hunter's office. She left the door open. She did not care who heard this.

"Ana . . . Hi," Hunter said cheerily. *Oh, he's guilty for sure*, Ana raged in her head.

"Hunter. What bullshit are you saying about me?" Ana asked outright, not feeling any sense of guilt at the accusatory tone she had.

"I don't know what you're talking about," he replied casually.

"If you said anything about me, Hunter, if I find out it was you that started this witch hunt against me, I'll . . . I'll . . ." Ana stammered.

"You'll what, Ana?" Hunter said, enjoying the view as he watched Ana shake with anger.

"I'll find out if it was you, Hunter. You think you're so clever, but I won't have you do this to me."

"I'm not doing anything to you, Ana. It's clear that you're handling everything just fine." He smirked at her, knowing it would just agitate her more.

"You're a pathetic, lonely man, and you're angry at me because I rejected you." Ana laughed.

"I'm not angry, Ana. Maybe it's you?" Hunter kept his cool and showed no signs of wavering from his nonchalant demeanor. But Ana saw his mouth twitch as if he were stopping himself from saying something he wanted to say. Ana turned on her heels and walked out. Just before she exited his office, she swirled around so quickly that Hunter barely had time to register her retort. "I am not angry. I am on the one happily married, and you are what? Still playing your little games with any woman that will give you attention? How pathetic are you?"

He could hear her laugh as she walked down the hall.

* * *

Darkness. The room was dark. Ana called out. *Was the electricity out?* She fumbled in the blackness of the room, trying to feel for a door, but she couldn't find one. The room was cold, empty. *Had she been robbed?* Ana felt her way forward as she took blind steps in front of her. She felt her teeth chatter from the sheer coldness. There was complete silence, an absence of life in the room. At first, she thought she was in her bedroom, but now, she did not have a clue. Ana rubbed her hands together, trying to feel some kind of warmth.

She continued to walk, uncertain of where she was going. While the darkness did not scare her, something within it did. What that was, she was not sure. But she felt like it was stalking her. She felt some sort of familiarity like she had been in this darkness before. And yet, she could not put her finger on it.

Ana tugged at her clothes. They felt wet, dirty, heavy. She felt weak, so tired like she had been walking forever. A flicker of light turned on in the distance. It shone bright, swaying in the wind Ana could not hear, but she could now feel. The light shone on, sharing its warmth with Ana every time the light hit her eyes. She reached out, trying to feel more of the warmth. But it only teased her, switching on and off, making her feel disorientated.

Ana broke into a sprint, feeling something looming behind her trying to frighten or intimidate her. With her hand outstretched, Ana focused on the light that went on and off. When she was close, when she could feel the warmth, it was blocked by a familiar figure: grandpa, with his wicked toothy smile and his dirty hands reaching out for her with the smell of grease. Ana stopped dead in her tracks. She could not move. She was paralyzed. Ana tried to scream, but as she opened her mouth, grandpa ran faster toward her. Within seconds, he had covered the remaining distance between them. Wrapping his long fingers across her mouth, the smell of oil made her want to vomit. He was trying to suffocate her. No . . . silence her . . .

Ana woke in a pool of her own sweat. Her heart was beating fast, a headache building within her temples. It had been a while since she had that dream, but it still brought so much fear within her. Ana shivered, turning toward Alexander who was peacefully asleep. Tears welled up in her eyes. She moved closer to Alexander, but he turned away. She knew it was the action of a sleeping man, but she suddenly felt alone again. Turning away from him too, Ana buried her face into her pillow and began sobbing like she was a six-year-old child again. Alone and afraid.

* * *

Back in the boardroom, Ana was presenting to the usual bunch of men who thought much more highly of their own voices than hers. Once again, she was telling them of the wins that were improving the profits of the business, but they were much more interested in ogling her body than in what she had to say. Hunter sat at the head of the table in direct view of Ana, the only one paying attention. It made Ana unusually nervous, aware she was being watched, monitored, and that anything she said or did would be reported.

Hunter whispered something to Greg, and he laughed, breaking up the boredom of the men. Greg yawned, causing the other men to laugh. Ana blushed.

"Maybe you could take your jacket off again? Show us some skin?" he teased. Hunter burst out laughing, encouraging him to continue. A few other men whistled at Ana.

"Yeah, Ana. Show us what makes the other men in the office go wild!" a colleague called out.

"Other men and I hear some other women too," winked another colleague. The men fell into a fit of laughter, deafening Ana's ears.

"This is inappropriate. Obviously, you didn't take my last warning seriously. That was your mistake!" Ana responded, raising her voice.

One of the men said, "Oh Ana, we are just playing."

Ana held her hand up to silence him and simply walked out of the room after saying her last words. "You'll be sorry you didn't listen the first time I warned you. This is sexual harassment, and it will go on all of your records. Ladies, I suggest you get up and go about your day and leave the good old boys here." Ana walked out with her head held high and the other women followed her. They were secretly very glad to be leaving that scene.

Alexander had booked a table at their favorite restaurant for lunch. Ana had been grateful to get out of the office for an hour to escape the looks, whispers, and gossip. Ana had burst into tears as she described the harassment she was receiving from her colleagues. It had been the same story as it had been the last few days, and Alexander sighed.

"I know it must be tough, Ana, but don't give them anything to fuel the fire." He patted her on the hand. Ana looked at him surprised. *Why was he not taking her side?*

"I don't give them fuel. They just keep throwing shit at me," Ana said through her tears.

"Okay, but just don't react. Don't rock the boat." Once again, Ana felt the sadness in her heart.

"Alexander, why are you talking to me like I'm a child?" she asked in frustration.

"I'm not, Ana. I am just saying that there's no winning this. Just sit quiet, say nothing, and it will pass."

Ana found herself wincing at his words. Had he done it on purpose? Repeating something her grandfather had said to Ana after one of his monstrous attacks on her. Ana pulled her hand away from Alexander as if the words burnt her skin. "How am I rocking the boat by being upset and finally taking a stance? I have a right to be upset about being sexually harassed at work," Ana replied angrily.

"Oh, come on, Ana. I'm not the enemy here. I'm just saying that you're being investigated already. You think it's not going to look strange if you file your own report?"

"So you're saying they won't believe me? That no one will believe me?" Ana knew she was having multiple conversations. Those fears of being a little child and feeling threatened into silence about the suffering she was enduring came back. This time, her husband was the one showing a lack of support in what she was going through. Ana tried not to take it out on him, but she couldn't help feeling angry at his lack of understanding. Ana looked away and resumed eating her food quietly, like the good little girl he said she should be. Alexander sighed and ate his food too. They ate the rest of their meal in silence.

* * *

Ana had been tucked in her office for most of the day. After her lunch with Alexander, she had not felt like socializing much. Her phone rang, but she ignored it. Alexander had been calling her for the past hour. She did not want to listen to whatever attempt of being "supportive" he had to offer. It felt very much to Ana like he was supporting their company much more than his wife, and after a lifetime of betrayal, she did not need yet another man to tell her to sit pretty and be quiet. Her voice mattered. Yet, the harder she tried to make it known, the more she was silenced.

The last few weeks of her life had tested her in ways she never thought she would be tested. She found herself thinking about Grace and whether she ever had to endure something like this. It made her miss her dear friend. Years of hard work to build a career seemed to be crumbling around her. She did not know if she could recover. Ana thought about all the men in her life, the ones who had beaten, cheated, and abused her. The ones who had made her feel worthless and alone. None of them had received the justice she had watched happen to the "bad guys" on TV. Where was the justice for every single time she had been pushed by a man who thought he could control her? She had fought all of her life to be somebody and the moment she finally felt like she had reached that, yet another man was trying to take it away from her.

Her desk phone rang. Ana did not recognize the number. Hesitantly, she answered the call.

"Ana . . ." It was Alexander. Ana sighed. Whatever he had to say better be good for him to go through so many channels to reach her. She had not even read his many emails.

"I've been fired."

Ana dropped her phone in shock, quickly picking up the receiver as she scrambled to gather whatever information she could from an upset Alexander. He had a history of delayed projects, but she knew Alexander was a perfectionist and could often spot mistakes from a mile away. This meant he would take much longer to complete work. Was the quality of work phenomenal? Yes, but as a boss herself, she knew how that could be challenging. Alexander's manager had told him that for this reason and a few other minor things, they had decided to let him go. They fired him without warning, without an official meeting, or without allowing him to fix the issues. He was expected to pack his bags and leave the building immediately.

The minor things ultimately led to a bigger problem they could not work through. Or so they told Alexander. But Ana knew deep down this had nothing to do with Alexander. It was just another underhanded way to get to her. She knew Hunter would be sitting at his desk right now enjoying every minute of her displeasure. Ana felt helpless, for herself and for Alexander. Hanging up, Alexander had told Ana he was headed home. Ana assured him she would be home as soon as possible. Alexander asked that she keep her head down, and she promised to do so.

Ana put her head on her table and began to cry. It was only a few short weeks ago that life felt so good. Like a sick joke, things had dramatically turned for the worse. It had been a long time since Ana had allowed herself to feel weak, but the realization that it was herself allowing this to happen gave her back her power.

Ana wiped her tears and kept her head down as Alexander had asked her. She stared at the clock, counting down the minutes until she could go home.

* * *

As she had expected, Alexander had been hit hard by losing his job. A job he had been in for ten years, a job he loved, a place he thrived in and knew so much about. Alexander was very much like Ana in that he made his job a major priority in his life, so it made sense to her for him to spiral. It had been three months since Alexander lost his job, and every day had been harder than the next. He had gone from having a glass of wine in the evenings to having champagne brunches, which turned into liquid breakfasts.

Ana did not remember the last time she had seen him sober and had expressed her concern to him, only to be met with anger and defiance. On many drunken outbursts, Alexander had outright blamed her for the misery he was in. Resentful, she kept her job when it was her scandals that had led to him losing his comfortable position within the company. Ana became angry each time he lost control and told her all the ways she had ruined his life. He was distant and had become a shadow of his former self.

That bright spark she had fallen in love with had dulled, but that only made her cling tighter to her husband, determined to get him back to how he was. Ana knew every hurtful thing he said was never personal, but it didn't stop her from falling into a deep depression.

With a husband emotionally checked out and mentally uninterested, it was easy for Ana to fall into a pattern of self-sabotage. She, too, had started drinking heavily, crying in private at every opportunity. Her passion for work had become something she fought to keep, but the reality was that she was living a nightmare at home and the torment she experienced every day at the hands of her colleagues. Still, she played nice, she kept her head above it all on the surface while inside she felt empty, broken, and betrayed.

To top it all off, Ana's nightly nightmares returned with a vengeance. Ana relived her childhood traumas every night again—the smell that haunted her, her grandfather, his hands, the garage, the wicked smile, and the men after that. Then her nightmares would transform into flashbacks of her toxic relationships over the years, relationships with other abusive men who had been in her life, especially Carter. This then brought back the countless other moments that made Ana want to give up, to let go, and disappear.

But she was not sixteen anymore. She couldn't just pick up her life and run away again. Haven was settled in her life with her husband and kids, kids Ana was very close to. If ever Ana felt alone, it was nothing compared to the moment Ana realized that for the first time in her life, she truly had no one in Seattle. Ana thought out loud, "Maybe it's time to go home and spend time with mom and Avery. At least they would understand." She knew how reckless she could be. After all the time she spent in therapy over the years, Ana could recognize the signs that she was about to sabotage herself. But sometimes, she was just too far gone. Sometimes life felt like it was just too hard on her, and all this betrayal might just be enough to break her.

Now the betrayal and sabotage she was experiencing from the team she trusted were too much to bear. They had all turned on her, and for what? Rumors. Ana could hardly believe this was happening, and her fear of losing everything was all too consuming. A few weeks back, her mom had come to visit, and while Alexander and Ana put on a good show of being okay, Sophia knew her daughter more than anyone. She feared Ana's self-sabotaging behavior was about to rear its ugly head. What was worse was the fact that Sophia couldn't stop it. Sure, she could make Ana aware of what she was seeing, and she did. But at the end of the day, Sophia saw her daughter go through these cycles a few times in her life. All Sophia could do was warn her, show support, and then worry day and night for her daughter.

* * *

At work, she passed the time by keeping busy and finishing projects. She would get home to darkness with Alexander passed out on the sofa littered with liquor bottles around him. Ana forgot the last time they had shared a meal together, let alone talked without fighting. *Was this what life was leading to?* Ana thought to herself. *Was this all that life would have to offer her—some great highs followed by the darkest lows? This story felt like it was on repeat in her life. She needed to stop the cycle but didn't know how without going to her old ways and she did not want that.*

Ana sat outside in the garden staring at the midnight sky. At what point was she meant to give up? She looked for a sign in the stars, but they twinkled in place. There was no answer for her up there. There was nothing telling her what to do. She felt like a little kid again, praying, hoping, and wishing for it all to make sense, wondering when it would be okay again like her mother had promised her.

* * *

Back in the boardroom, Ana found herself staring into space as Hunter presented the company expansion to the senior team. She was not listening. He did not want any of their input. This meeting was more for boosting his ego and showing off rather than having any real substance. Hunter did not care about their opinion. He felt and acted as if he was untouchable.

Hunter could see Ana was not paying attention. A surge of anger rose in him at her constant defiance, as if she still had not learned what it meant for her when she challenged him.

"And of course, bigger profits, bigger teams, stronger companies mean better benefits. Plenty of time for you all to go on company trips and have hot tub threesomes. Right, Ana?" Hunter publicly sharing the latest rumor from her last well deserved paid company retreat. *A threesome*, she scoffed thinking about just how crazy the incident sounded when she first heard it a few weeks back from Zack.

The team burst into disorganized laughter. Ana could see the anger in his eyes. For the first time, she was actually scared of him and of what he could do to her.

Ana ignored it and politely smiled. He could not hurt her any more than he already had. She would not dignify his joke with a comment. She did not want to give him the satisfaction of letting on that he hurt her. It was clear she was in a man's world, and she needed to just keep to herself.

The meeting continued with Hunter bringing the men alive with naughty jokes and inappropriate comments. Zack came into the last part of the meeting, and for the first time in a while, Ana was thankful for him showing up. It meant everyone had to be on their best behavior.

A few snide remarks still managed to slip past him, causing Ana to feel the anger prickle her skin. Finally, the meeting finished, and as Ana made her way out of the boardroom, Hunter called after her. "Ana . . ." Instinctively, she turned to acknowledge him. "Do give our best to Alexander." He winked at her, causing the men to laugh once again. Ana picked up the water pitcher. She wanted to throw it at his smug face. She could quite easily do it. Instead, she threw it to the ground, her anger no longer contained. The glass smashed into tiny pieces, one stray shard scratching her face and drawing blood. The room fell into silence as Zack pulled her out of the room and into his office. Ana took a gulp of air as the anger inside her dissipated, finding herself falling apart much like the jug. Ana looked down knowing what was to come.

She sat in his office. Zack sat at his desk like a principal punishing a misbehaving student. Zack was her only friend left in the office. In his presence, she felt a sense of calm wash over her. Zack had finally seen firsthand what the animals in the boardroom were like. Surely, he must now realize all of the lies spread about her!

Ana looked to Zack, but he was not there. The kind, caring mentor, her friend, and all traces of his gentle kindness were gone; he was gone. The only Zack that was left was Hunter's Zack, manipulated into believing the lies, the problems Ana apparently left in her wake. He opened his mouth to speak, Ana knew what was coming, her head was pounding, the white noise filling her ears was deafening.

"I'm sorry, Ana. I'm letting you go." Zack mumbled.
* * *

Wiping clean the dried blood on her face, Ana ordered another double whisky. The bar was practically empty in the early afternoon. She had been fired. She had packed her bags and walked out of the office with her head held high. Inside, she was breaking, shattering. The shock was only starting to wear off after her fourth glass. But still, she was shaking. Anger seeped into her blood.

How dare another man try to ruin her? How could she have been fired without provocation? The "investigation" Zack had promised never truly happened. All they did was talk to a few "guys." She knew where that was going. How did her life get to a point where yet another person felt entitled enough to break the confidence she had worked so hard to build?

She hated Hunter, Zack, her grandfather, and sadly now, her husband. Yes, she could finally admit it. She hated Alexander. She hated the way he blamed her for every single thing wrong in his life when she had brought so much good into it. She hated the way he had allowed the demon inside him to take over, to turn to drinking instead of turning to his wife. He had all but abandoned her, emotionally abused her, let her carry on paying the bills, all while berating her for the way she conducted herself. Ana had pleaded with him too many times to count to get help, get off the couch, to stop drinking, but it all fell on deaf ears. To him, everything was her fault. Nothing was going to change how he felt.

For all of Ana's life, she had allowed everyone to have a say in her life but herself. Taking another sip of her drink, Ana felt her anger flow throughout her body. She was drunk and raging. All she wanted was a safe place to be able to navigate through the stress of work without the bullying she was enduring. She had fought to the bitter end, allowed herself to be graceful and silent, but it did not pay off.

She did as Alexander had asked—every day at work, she behaved and wore her work mask, smiled, and then once arriving home, put on the pretty wife mask. She didn't feel like he appreciated her effort. She had held his hand, cried with him, reminded him of every good quality he had, and when she needed her husband, he was nowhere to be found. He had checked out of the marriage, and she wondered why she had not done the same. She loved him. But loving him was causing her to lose herself. She was forgetting the strength she had built within herself, the resilience wearing thin. If he loved her, why was he hurting her like this and not supporting her? She knew the answer: he was too lost in his own grief to see hers. Every man had taken something from her, slowly leaving her with nothing. Ana forgot what it felt like to be confident, to feel good, and she was willing to give anything to get that back.

The bartender cleared the empty glasses around her, replacing them with a full glass in front of her. She looked up at him. His hazel eyes gave a glint of mischievousness that she recognized from back in her party days. Ana smiled at him, thinking about what it would feel like to have his tanned and toned skin pressing against hers. Taking another sip, she watched as he worked effortlessly to make a cocktail. She liked the way he handled the mixer, carefully making art in front of her. Their eyes flirted. He looked at her the way she liked to be admired. Ana knew, at that moment, that she was going to do bad things to him. Ana leaned over the bar and pulled him by his shirt, putting her lips against him. He tasted of something sweet. Her tongue explored his mouth a little longer before pulling away. Silently, Ana beckoned for him to come to her, but instead, he gestured for her to follow him. Obligingly, she did, going into the back office. He lifted her up on the table and undressed her. Impatiently, she pulled off his shirt and kissed his muscled chest. He pulled a condom out of his pocket and Ana watched him as he unzipped his pants and rolled it on. Closing her eyes, Ana let the drink lead her as their bodies came together.

* * *

Ana was the queen of self-sabotage and felt unlovable. Troubled Ana left a path of destruction because she knew all too well that no one could hurt her more than she hurt herself, no matter what mask she tried to hide behind.

Laying in her empty tub, Ana cried to herself. Both outside and inside, a storm was brewing. Ana wiped away her tears. It had been a few weeks since her tryst with the random bartender. She had been tiptoeing around what she had done, afraid to admit how she had broken her vows as she avoided her husband, but right now, she needed him. She walked to the living room where Alexander was sitting, watching trashy TV, nursing a hangover while drinking his fourth beer for the day. Ana sat beside him, getting ready to share herself with him.

Ana talked slowly and quietly as she discussed the pain she was feeling. Alexander did not lift his eyes away from the TV, but she continued talking. The loss of her job, while not affecting Alexander, had hurt her deeply. She talked about how they were both falling apart and how she could no longer be the strong one for both of them. "Do you even hear me, Alexander?" Ana asked him quietly. She was met with nothing, again.

"I need my husband." Ana began to cry, wanting to reach the depth of him that she knew still existed. She wanted the man who had once made her laugh, danced with her in the kitchen when no music played, the man she had seen beautiful places with. Their beautiful home was in constant darkness. They both hid from each other. She hated him for his weakness, while at the same time, she painfully loved him.

Frustrated by the silence, Ana finally told him of her indiscretion. She could not bring herself to say affair because it had been a one-time thing. Since then, she had been racked with guilt, going so far as to avoid sleeping in the same bed as her husband.

Alexander remained silent but looked up at her, his vision slightly blurred. "I'm sorry, Alexander," Ana said quietly, sobbing into her hands. He reached out and touched her knee, gentle, careful, almost like he was trying to reclaim the old Alexander back again.

"I forgive you," he mumbled, tears filling his eyes. Together they cried, holding hands, holding each other, finally unified as man and woman by the pain they held inside themselves.

Ana knew in her heart that her fighting for their marriage was futile. The man who had once given her so much love was now putting her through so much pain. Something Grace had once said came to mind: "Love isn't meant to be that hard, and if it is, then it isn't love." She was right, love shouldn't be this hard. Ana had never known an easy love, or at least, she could not remember if there was ever a time when it was easy. It had been a long few months of Ana being the bad guy, and every time Alexander looked at her, he saw the face of the person who had contributed to the spiral of his mental health.

Ana resented him. They were married, but it had been a long time since they felt like they were together. Alexander could not get his head out of the darkness that he had fallen into. As much as Ana tried to bring normality into their lives, he had begun drowning her in his sorrows. Ana was strong, but with Alexander, she now felt weak. She had allowed herself to indulge in the sadness, to let herself become convinced that the world was just as evil as it had been when she was a child. They had become toxic for each other, but it was the fighter inside Ana that refused to let go of him. Every time she felt like she wanted to give up, he would come back and say something profound that would stop her in her tracks. He forgave her affair, forgave her for breaking her vows. The skeptical side of Ana thought about how it was all due to her being his life raft. He used her will to survive as a safety device when he should have been using his sheer love for her.

Ana felt trapped. She had hoped that he would hate her, shout at her, break out of the spell of misery he was in, but instead, he accepted it. He accepted what she had done, and part of her thanked him for it.

Alexander kissed Ana on her lips. She didn't want him. She tasted the alcohol in his mouth and smelled the alcohol on his skin, but still, she allowed him to feel the closeness he sought for. Going to bed together, they made love. Their tear-stained faces reflected the emotions and love they felt. They let their guards down to allow for just a moment of peace.

His breath smelled of smoke and alcohol. Breathing on her neck, he licked her skin. He felt his way up her leg toward her thigh and played with the band of her underwear. Ana felt scared. Shivering from the cold of the metal on her bare legs, she closed her eyes. She felt his lips, dry and chapped. His fingers spread black grease stains on her delicate skin.

He put his dirty hands on her mouth, pressing forcefully down on her face, trying to silence her, but instead suffocated her. Ana opened her eyes. She stared at him, her grandpa with his wild eyes. He was drunk again. She could see the way his body was swaying, unable to steady himself. He pulled down her underwear as she screamed into his hand. He smiled as she tried to squirm away. The crookedness in his face etched into her mind. *Please stop*, Ana thought to herself, pleading with her eyes. *Grandpa, please stop*, she silently begged.

* * *

Ana shot up, waking up from a deep sleep. Frantic, she clutched at her face, wiping away the grease that had covered her in her dreams. Realizing it was just another nightmare, Ana steadied her breath. Alexander was sound asleep beside her, facing away again as far from her as possible on their king-sized bed.

It had been a series of sleepless nights. The days were starting to roll into each other. Ana tiptoed out of bed and made her way into her home office. Sitting at her desk, she turned on her screen. Her computer came to life as she began researching employment rights.

It had been some time since she was fired, her inappropriate behavior being used as reasoning. The harassment and bullying she had experienced were never once taken into consideration. Ana had allowed herself to be embarrassed out of a job she had worked so hard for, losing clients that she had secured of her own merit and sheer talent. She had made millions for the company, and yet, she was treated like nothing she'd done had mattered. When they finally couriered the rest of her office belongings, all the awards she'd earned had been broken.

Ana wiped the tears falling down her cheek. She would be a victim no more. Fuck Hunter, fuck Zack, fuck Alexander's advice to sit pretty and shrug it off. She needed to stand up for what was right. For the first time, she was going to seek justice. She was going to fight back.

She had worked tirelessly researching her legal rights. The law jargon confused and exhausted her at first, but not nearly as much as the injustices she'd faced in life. She was going to take back her dignity.

Ana stopped seeing herself as an individual victim and instead found herself pouring over the hundreds of cases of women being harassed at work. On many occasions, these women went unheard, just as she went unheard as a little girl. She was abused by a family member who was supposed to protect and love her, then was let down by a system made to protect her. Now, as an adult, she no longer wanted to rely on anyone to do the fighting for her. For once, she was going to gain control instead of being shamed into silence. Anastasia wanted to fight for what was right. Not only for her but for the hundreds and thousands of other women who had been beaten down and broken by the corporate world that protected the overly paid men who ruled it.

It was Ana's time to use her voice, her power, and her experience to shatter the glass ceiling and expose a toxic workplace culture that she had once accepted. For her whole life, Ana cared about people and advocated passionately for diversity and inclusion, her values were strong. She was going to stand up for those things that had always mattered to her, and she was going to do this for her and for all the other women. Most of all, Ana wanted justice for the little girl inside her who had tried to use her voice for good and was punished through alienation and fear. The strength she felt grew as she learned more about what she could do to get the justice she deserved.

Hunter, Greg, and even Zack deserved to be punished for what they did and allowed. They picked at every weakness Ana had and used it to create a monster in the eyes of her colleagues. The one thing they did not count on was the nerve she had to fight back. Feeling empowered after the research she had done, Ana was ready to take it on. *Let's play, boys!*

* *

Ana walked into the courtroom with her head held high. She had been working hard for months finding the right lawyer, spending countless nights scouring the internet about employment law, and gathering the evidence she needed for her case.

She watched as those who had hurt her, abused her, belittled her, and fired her shamefully walk into the courtroom after her. Ana kept reminding herself to use her emotions to make her strong for once, just like when she was twelve years old when she pushed aside her own emotional well-being to finally share her truth for the sake of protecting the ones she loved.

Ana wondered whether this was what her mother had to go through all those years ago when she had to bear witness to her own father, Ana's grandfather, pleading guilty for the abuse he put Ana through in her childhood. She wondered whether her mom had felt the nerves too, whether she was afraid to look at the abuser, or whether part of her felt shame even if she should not.

Taking deep breaths, Ana allowed herself to watch the court proceedings through her professional view. Watching as the men were questioned, Ana was uncomfortable by the truth coming out and the evident disregard for her well-being as she was subjected to sexist bullying and unlawful investigation into her private life. She reveled as the judge read out the breach of contract and every wrong action that happened while she was employed under their guidance.

She secretly enjoyed watching the men, who once stood tall and proud, cowered at the punishment handed to them as the company she was not protected by was found guilty of the treatment she received. They had to answer for unfair dismissal, sexual harassment, bullying, defamation of character, and a serious list of misconduct. Most importantly, the policies within the company were old and were there to protect the offenders. Now, they would be rewritten and approved under the laws that governed that court.

In just a few hours, Ana was given the justice she had been waiting for, receiving a large payout for the lost wages and emotional suffering. But the justice received for the defamation of her character was the icing on the cake for her. There was much more satisfaction in knowing that for the first time in her life, she was able to gain control and finally receive the justice she deserved.

She could look at one of her abusers knowing she had won. Ana stood to get up at the same time Hunter started to leave. They crossed paths as he glared at her. Ana smiled back at him. She allowed him no words, just a wink. Ana knew she had outsmarted him once and for all.

Elation filled Ana's body as she knew she had won for the many women who did not get their day in court. Finally, she could celebrate the first bit of victory she had experienced in her life. Hugging each of her lawyers, she thanked them for their support, grateful to each of them for holding her hand through the questioning and believing her. Just as she was about to walk out of the court, she saw something in the corner of her eye that stopped her dead in her tracks—Grace. She was sitting there all alone being a silent supporter. Ana immediately dropped her purse and ran over and gave her friend a hug. No words were needed. Ana had texted her that morning, but she never thought she'd show up.

"Want to grab a coffee, Anastasia?" was all Grace said, with a big beaming smile on her face. The two ladies left arm in arm.

Ana used her voice to rise above her abusers. She had stood up for herself. For once, the bad guys did not get away with what they did, and that was all Anastasia was after—justice. Ana smiled as she drove home, excited to share her good news. She hoped it would finally help bring Alexander out from his depression.

* * *

For old times' sake, Ana walked through the front door with a huge smile on her face. "Babe, I'm home!" she shouted, unable to contain her excitement. She walked into the kitchen. Instead of the delicious home-cooked meal that once welcomed her home, the kitchen counter was littered with takeout containers and empty liquor bottles.

Alexander was sitting at the table waiting for her, his beard scraggly and his hair unkempt. But, at least today, he was dressed. Ana beamed at him. "I have great news!" She smiled, trying not to be deterred by his disheveled appearance. Ana raised her hand as she showed him a bottle of non-alcoholic fizzy cider she had bought for them to celebrate with.

Alexander tried to force a smile without losing his nerve. He looked at Ana's happy face and sighed. "Ana . . . I'm sorry, but I don't love you anymore."

The words burned so much that Ana lost her composure and dropped the cider to smash into a million pieces on the marble floor. The loud noise of the bottle crashing onto the floor echoed through the room. But Ana heard none of it in her state of shock.

He cleared his throat, ignoring the mess and her loud sobs as she tried to grasp the situation. Her elation quickly disappeared. She felt utter despair. Alexander looked away from Ana, unable to look at her in her emotional state a moment longer. He took a deep breath.

"I want a divorce."

Chapter 14

Ana sat on the floor of her bathroom. It had been three weeks since Alexander had made his earth-shattering announcement. For the first two days, Ana could do nothing but sob uncontrollably. She missed her life, her job, and her husband. She wanted to wave a magic wand and go back to the fairy tale where everything was magical again. If she'd had that wand, maybe she'd go back even further to make sure her grandfather never touched her. She'd ensure that she would never have to carry all of the baggage that had caused her to be impulsive or interested in men like Carter and Hunter because of her need for the wrong kind of male attention. But if she did that, she never would have met Alexander and had some of the happiest moments of her life. No, she wouldn't trade that.

Haven knocked on the bathroom door. "Ana?"

Anthony's voice soon followed. "Ana? Can we come in?"

Ana reached up to open the door and saw her two closest friends. They hadn't abandoned her at least. When she finally stopped crying and was able to sleep, the nightmares had started again, then sleep became impossible. Haven had come by a few days later after not hearing from her and let herself in with the spare key. She'd found Ana, curled up on the sofa with dark circles under her red-rimmed eyes. Haven had moved into the guest bedroom that night. When Ana finally fell asleep and cried out, Haven crawled in bed with her and didn't let go.

The next day, Haven had called in Anthony for reinforcements. He had a friend who swore by herbal supplements for sleep and nightmares, and he was over at her house with boxes of the stuff under each arm within the hour. Seeing him in her kitchen looking like a package boy was the first time Ana had laughed in what felt like years.

They had cared for her as much as they could. Slowly, she started feeling like herself again. The nightmares receded, and she found a certain comfort in the rhythm of her day. She knew Haven and Anthony couldn't completely leave their lives behind for her, but she had been so grateful for their unconditional love and support. It was something she'd needed so badly that it made her bones ache. Her mother called every day and was also a great help as Sophia always knew when she needed to vent or when she needed real advice. Dad, Trisha, and Avery called every few days as well. Ana felt blessed to have the family she did, but they couldn't make it better for her; she had to.

She knew she was feeling better when Anthony had convinced her to go on a shopping spree and a lunch date. Although Haven and Anthony were both in committed relationships, it didn't stop them from ogling and pointing out beautiful men to Ana on their outing.

"You two never change, do you?" She laughed at them.

They looked at each other in mock offense. "No! And I hope we never do," Anthony answered.

"Me either."

They'd gone to their favorite bar at the end of the day, but Ana had felt off at lunch and wasn't feeling much better now. Her stomach felt queasy, and her lunch had tasted funny. The martini she sipped on tasted more like dirt than anything else.

"Ana?" Anthony looked at her worried. "You okay?"

Ana rubbed her head. She felt flushed and dizzy as beads of sweat raised on her forehead. "I think I may need to go home. Sorry to ruin the celebration of our outing."

Haven waved her off while Anthony paid the bill.

At home, Haven tucked her into bed. Ana rolled her eyes at her hovering over her like a mother hen, but secretly she was glad for both their presence and concern.

"Haven, I'm fine, really. It's probably just stress." Ana tried to wave her off, but Haven insisted. She gathered her friend's head in her lap and stroked her hair.

"Stress? You've been under stress? I didn't notice."

Ana swatted at her lovingly and leaned into Haven's touch. "It has been a nasty few months, hasn't it? And to think, not that long ago I was on top of the world, living the dream and thinking nothing could upset that balance."

"I think we all feel that way before we step into the bullshit," Anthony chimed in from the door.

"You look a little green, Ana. You sure you're okay?"

The queasiness had suddenly turned into full-on nausea. Ana threw off her blankets and ran for the bathroom. After she cleaned herself up a bit, she felt surprisingly better.

When Ana walked back into the bedroom, her friends were sharing mutual looks of concern and furrowed brows.

"Ana . . ." Haven started. "Could you be . . . ?"

Realization hit Ana like a ton of bricks. *It wasn't possible. Was it?* She tried to mentally calculate when her last period had been but admittedly hadn't been keeping very good track during all of the courtroom drama. She remembered the last time she and Alexander had sex. The smell of the alcohol. The fleeting moment of peace.

"I don't know."

"Well, we'll let you get some rest and figure something out tomorrow."

Which is how she came to be sitting on her bathroom floor with her friends hovering outside. Anthony had gone to the nearest store and picked out as many pregnancy tests as he could find. Two of them sat on the counter.

Haven crouched down next to Ana. "It's been three minutes. Do you want me to look?"

Ana shook her head. "No. I can do it."

Haven helped her stand up and Ana walked over to the bathroom counter. She peered into the window of both tests. The pink lines on one glared back at her, while the other test shouted "Pregnant" in bold letters.

Haven and Anthony stood behind her. "Oh, Ana," Haven whispered.

"I'm going to take a bath. Will you guys stay for a little bit?" She turned to both of them and held their hands.

"Of course," Anthony hugged her and patted her back.

While Ana ran the water, she thought about what it would mean to bring a baby into the world. What it would mean for her world. Was she capable of raising a child on her own? She had witnessed the evil of men and the world first-hand. *What if she had a daughter that experienced the same thing? What if she raised a boy that was no better than Hunter? What if any child she had was preyed upon like she was?* She couldn't handle the thought of that happening.

She knew she couldn't think like that. It wouldn't do her any good to dwell on that kind of toxicity. She thought about her mom, Avery, Dad, Trisha, Grace, Haven, and Anthony. All the people that loved her and had done their best to stand by her. With any luck, any child she brought into the world would be like any one of them. The silver lining was that at least she knew the signs and knew that monsters lurked where you least expected them.

Motherhood was something that she had thought about in passing in the good moments, but she'd felt like she still had more to accomplish in her career and more time to spend with Alexander before they made that decision. Now all of that had been taken from her, but what about everything that she might gain as a mother?

This is going to be one hell of a journal entry, she thought to herself.

The warm water enveloping her calmed her. She thought about all the journals she'd kept for so long. She'd held onto them like a lifeline. They were proof, validation of her feelings and what she'd gone through over the years. There was hurt, pain, anger, happiness, elation, wins, all etched on their pages in indelible ink. There hadn't been a day that had gone by where she hadn't filled at least two pages with what had happened that day.

Maybe this was a fresh start. Maybe this was her opportunity to finally create something lasting and real. Someone that she could love unconditionally. Someone to protect and build a life with. *Maybe this was the real fairy tale she was meant to have.*

Ana cupped her hands over her stomach and imagined the life blossoming inside of her. This was hers. This was something no one could take away from her. This would give her the strength to continue fighting for a world where injustice doesn't win.

Ana got up and toweled herself off. She put on her robe and looked at herself in the mirror. *Who would have thought the love I so desperately was chasing with all those men was within me the whole time?* She smiled looking back at herself. Her skin was glowing from the heat of the bathwater. She walked into her living room, past Haven and Anthony. Rows of her journals were lined on her bookshelf in chronological order.

"Anthony, would you do me a favor and grab the matches from the drawer in the kitchen? Haven, will you help me with these please?"

Ana started pulling the journals from the shelves. She walked into the backyard toward the firepit that was situated in the center of the patio. She dumped an armful of the journals in.

"Ana, your journals? Are you sure about this?"

Feeling lighter than she had in years, Ana turned to her friend and smiled. "I've never been more sure about anything. I need to let go of that other me."

Haven smiled back. "Okay, then. Let's do this."

They cleared the shelves of every single journal. Ana kept only one. A brand new one with fresh pages and no ink. It was time to write a new story. This was her chance to let go of the past and create a better, beautiful future for herself and her unborn child.

Anthony handed her the matches. "Would you like to do the honors?"

The box of matches felt cool in her hand. Ana hesitated.

"Actually, if you guys don't mind, I think I need to do this myself. Will you wait here?"

Anthony and Haven each hugged her. "Of course, we will."

The three of them stacked the journals as well as they could for Ana to carry, and she made her way down to her favorite place on the beach below her house. She set the journals down to make a mini firepit and then carefully set the journals on top. She opened the box of matches and took a deep breath. She struck one and set the flame to the edge of one of the journals and watched it smoke before the flame caught. Ana stood back with her hands gently holding her stomach as she watched in peaceful silence as all the old memories went up in flames. Her new story was going to be one of love, peace, and patience. She was going to do things in her own time and her own way.

While Ana watched her journals burn, she heard a small voice in her head asking how she felt. For some reason, she thought it sounded like Grace. Ana was sitting on a rock near the water's edge and said to her growing baby, "You and I are going to have a great life because I love you unconditionally already."

Ana sat for a while watching them burn. It was therapeutic for her to see each page curl into the red flames and turn to ash; a reminder that her past could just as easily be let go and she could be forgiven. As the sun started to set and the journals turned to embers, she walked along the beach with her feet in the water imagining the childhood she would give her growing baby. She had never felt so at peace than in this moment and for the first time in a long time, the inner peace she felt so deeply told her that everything was going to be as she always hoped for. She lived in the home of her dreams right on the water, she had the unconditional love of her family and friends, and most importantly she grew to love herself and now had the experience and confidence to know she could make it in this world alone, but now she was not alone, she has her unborn child, *her baby*.

About the Author

Gina E. Matteson has been on her own journey of self-discovery and self-love. She founded GemTek in February 2020 and has fallen in love with business again. After over twenty years in the Recruitment and HR field, she is finally living and working by her own standards and moral compass.

Gina now lives back in her home country of Canada, with her husband, Gary, and their two children, Connor and Charlotte. She is a successful CEO, mother, and wife. *A Thousand Masks* is inspired by true events and is her debut novel.

Connect with Gina:
www.ginamatteson.com
Instagram: @authorginamatteson
LinkedIn: Gina Matteson

Lightning Source UK Ltd.
Milton Keynes UK
UKHW012159190422
401727UK00002B/506